Before she knew what he was doing, he stooped and kissed her.

She wasn't expecting it, wasn't prepared. So without thought she kissed him back. For a minute they were back in Majorca, hiding in the shadows of the garden, snatching a moment of illicit pleasure. But then she pushed him away.

They were close; she could see the turmoil in his eyes and wondered what he could see in hers.

Gill Sanderson, aka Roger Sanderson, started writing as a husband-and-wife team. At first Gill created the storyline, characters and background, asking Roger to help with the actual writing. But her job became more and more time-consuming and he took over all of the work. He loves it! Roger has written many Medical Romance™ books for Harlequin Mills & Boon®. Ideas come from three of his children—Helen is a midwife, Adam a health visitor, Mark a consultant oncologist. Weekdays are for work; weekends find Roger walking in the Lake District or Wales.

Recent titles by the same author:

EMERGENCY: BACHELOR DOCTOR
A FATHER'S SPECIAL CARE
THE CONSULTANT'S RESCUE

A DOCTOR TO COME HOME TO

BY
GILL SANDERSON

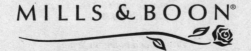
MILLS & BOON®

All the characters in this book have no existence outside the imagination of the author, and have no relation whatsoever to anyone bearing the same name or names. They are not even distantly inspired by any individual known or unknown to the author, and all the incidents are pure invention.

First published in Great Britain 2004
Harlequin Mills & Boon Limited,
Eton House, 18-24 Paradise Road, Richmond, Surrey TW9 1SR

© Gill Sanderson 2004

ISBN 0 263 83942 7

Set in Times Roman 10½ on 12¼ pt.
03-1204-47973

Printed and bound in Spain
by Litografia Rosés, S.A., Barcelona

CHAPTER ONE

AFTERWARDS, Amy Harrison remembered how she had felt earlier that morning. Not really happy, not really contented, but more or less at peace with the world. She had her friends, she lived in one of the most beautiful and unspoiled districts of Britain, she had the job of District Nurse, which she loved. She had her four-year-old daughter Elizabeth. She could cope with her life, deal with its disappointments.

Then Dr Adam Ross had marched back into that life. And things weren't peaceful any more.

Like on all work days, she had started early. As well as herself there was Elizabeth to bathe and give breakfast to. Then a short drive round to her mother's to drop Elizabeth off. Amy thought herself lucky that she had found the house she wanted, so close to her mother. She was even more lucky that her mother was a registered childminder.

Elizabeth loved being with her nan, and played happily with the other three children that Amy's mother looked after. The house rang with the noise of children enjoying themselves, it always felt happy. Amy knew that Elizabeth couldn't be in better hands, and that made her life, well, possible.

It was easy to drive out of the little Derbyshire town of Lissom. It was a gorgeous October day, and soon Amy was driving along a valley, through the mist that rose from the river. Her heart lifted with the beauty of it. This was why she stayed in Derbyshire!

She watched for the narrow entrance, turned into the lane that led up to Top Clough Farm. It was a steep, bumpy, rattling ride, the heather brushed the side of her car and she was glad of the four-wheel-drive.

So, it was halfway through October. In a couple of weeks the clocks would go back. It would be time for parties, Hallowe'en, Bonfire Night. Basically, party time for children. She would help her mother organise something for those in her charge. There was also often something organised at the surgery for the staff. She supposed she'd have to go. It would be good to spend time with friends—but she wasn't one for parties. Not any more.

Ahead, above, was Top Clough Farm, a scattering of grey buildings on the shoulder of a green hill. A hard place to earn a living, but beautiful in its own stark way.

Amy drove into the farmyard, checked the state of the ground and decided it wasn't yet necessary to put on the Wellington boots she always carried in the back of the car. All right now, but in December…

As she walked across the yard she heard the hum of machinery coming from the shippen. She peered in the door. Alan Dunnings was checking the leads to the milking parlour. Amy knew him quite well, having been at school with him.

'Amy! Good to see you. Come to give Dad a check-up?'

'Just the usual, thought I'd call in. How has he been?'

Alan came to the door, shaking his head. 'I'm going to have to tie him down, Amy. The minute I turn my back he starts on something. I was clearing a ditch on the back pasture last week and he was supposed to go on a short walk, like you said. I came back to find him mending a wall in the paddock. Dry-stone walling, Amy! He looked as grey as the limestone he was handling.'

'I'll have another word with him,' Amy promised. 'He just can't act this way.'

'Tell him,' said Alan.

Alan was supposed to work in partnership with his father, Alf. Alf's wife Mavis had died two years ago. The two men had got on well together—until Alf had fallen ill. He'd had a heart attack. There had been a sudden desperate rush to hospital, emergency treatment. Now Alf was home again—but never again would he work as he had done.

Amy knocked, then walked straight into the stone-floored kitchen. Alf looked up from the book he was reading then leapt to his feet. 'Amy! Let me pour you a cup of tea, I've just—'

Amy placed a hand on his chest, eased him back into his chair. 'I'll pour my own tea,' she said. 'I can see the teapot. You sit there and take things easy. What's this about dry-stone walling? I thought we agreed that you'd take things easy.'

'I've worked all my life. I'm not stopping now.'

'You're not stopping, you're just to do less. How d'you feel?'

'I'm OK. I…' He looked at Amy's stern face and then said, 'I've felt better.'

'Not surprising. Now, let's have a look at you.'

Quickly Amy listened to his chest, took the other readings that were standard. Then, carefully, she wrote down the results. Note-keeping was all-important. Only then did she pour herself a mug of tea and sit opposite Alf.

'This is serious, Alf. You're not as good as you were when I called a fortnight ago—you're going backwards because you won't rest and wait.'

'Top Clough has always been a tidy farm. If I see something wrong, I put it right.'

She sighed. This was not something she liked doing, but she had to. She had to get through to him.

'You're tough, we know that. The heart attack you had would have killed a lot of men. But what you have to do is take things easy, and in another couple of months you can start on some light work. But if you have another attack like last time—well, you won't come out of hospital and come straight back up here. You'll have to spend the rest of your life in some kind of sheltered accommodation down in town. Probably in a wheelchair.'

She saw the panic in his eyes, felt guilty for what she had said. But it was the truth. So she went on, more gently, 'But it doesn't have to come to that if you look after yourself. Going to do what I say?'

'I'll do what you say.'

'Good. Because I want to keep on coming up here. Now, tell me about those sheep I saw in the bottom meadow...'

'He'll pay more attention to you than to me,' Alan said to her fifteen minutes later, as she re-crossed the farmyard. 'Have you talked sense into him?'

Amy could see the concern in the man's eyes. 'I've

tried,' she said. 'I'll not leave it so long before I come again—I'll try to drop in next week.'

'We both appreciate that.' Alan handed her a bottle. 'Cream,' he said, 'fresh this morning. Put it on Elizabeth's cornflakes.'

'And on mine. Thanks, Alan, I'll be seeing you.'

As she bounced back down the track she thought that visiting people like the Dunnings was what made the job worthwhile.

The rest of her morning's jobs were in the town itself. First she called on Elsie Pennant, who lived in a tiny terrace house on the outskirts of town. Elsie had scalded her leg badly while making her early morning tea. Amy changed the dressing, then helped Elsie have a wash. This gave them a chance to catch up on gossip. Amy noticed that Elsie seemed more frail than usual, and perhaps more forgetful. That often happened after a trauma. Amy made a mental note to get in touch with Social Services. Perhaps a preliminary interview was needed.

Then there were two sets of injections to be given, again older people who could not be relied upon to inject themselves. These were over quickly. The next patient was very different.

Travis Kay, a keen and apparently expert climber, had fallen while climbing a local rockface, Stanage Edge. He had a compound fracture of one leg and very deep lacerations. Travis was not taking kindly to having to stay immobile.

His wife let Amy in, a resigned expression on her face. 'You try to stop him, I can't,' she said. 'I'm only his wife.'

Amy could hear grunting, gasping noises from the front room, which had been converted into a temporary bedroom. She knocked, peered round the door then blinked. Was she seeing things?

Travis's bed was in the middle of the room. Above it was a metal construction—it looked home-made but sturdy. From it Travis was hanging, his muscular arms pulling him upwards, his plaster-clad leg stuck out clumsily in front. When he saw Amy he slowly lowered himself onto the bed. 'Got to keep fit,' he said. 'The lads built this for me. A gym for the bed-bound.'

Amy grinned. 'Fall on that leg again and you'll really be in trouble,' she said. 'Travis, can't you just for once stay still for a few days?'

'It's hard,' Travis said. 'Amy, I get so bored.'

'Well, I've warned you. Fall badly and you're in real trouble. Now, let's have a look at that cast.'

Travis seemed to be getting better. If he fell on that leg he could cause himself a lot of trouble. But he seemed happier now he had something to do, some way of exercising. Amy decided that she wouldn't be putting forward Travis's construction as suitable for everyone with a broken leg, but if it made Travis an easier patient, it was good.

So, quite a typical morning. She enjoyed it. A mix of people, the feeling that you were helping someone, always something new to talk about. There were far worse jobs than being a district nurse.

At lunchtime she drove back to the Riverside Surgery, to which she was attached. Technically, she didn't work there, that was the job of the practice nurse. But they all worked together—well.

This afternoon she was going to help out with the flu vaccinations for the older people in the district. There would be a queue of patients waiting to come in, but the job was simple. It was almost like a factory production line—people bared their arms outside, came in, gave their names and less than a minute later were out of the door again. But it was valuable work.

But that was this afternoon. Now Amy had chance to get her records straight, have a bite of lunch, perhaps even slip into town to do some shopping.

As she entered the car park she noticed a new car in the doctors' area—a maroon Range Rover. Vaguely she wondered whose it could be. There had been talk in the practice about getting a locum. Annie Best, their one female doctor, had taken six months off to have her first baby, and things had been very busy without her. It had been hard to find a suitable locum—not a lot of doctors wanted to come to work in a small Derbyshire town.

Amy took her sandwiches and briefcase and let herself in. First, a quick trip to the cloakroom to brush out her short dark hair, rub the mud from her shoes and in general make herself look respectable. Then she frowned at her reflection. Her uniform looked a bit loose on her, a bit baggy. She went into the treatment room and weighed herself—nine pounds under what she thought was her best weight. Wryly, she wondered what she was complaining about. Most women had difficulty keeping weight off, not putting it on. She would try to eat a little more. If she remembered.

So far just a normal day. She had enjoyed what she

had done but it was a day like so many others. And then things changed.

She was walking across the reception area, looking forward to her sandwiches and tea, and catching up with news, when a young female voice behind her called out, 'Amy—it's Amy. Oh, it's so good to see you!'

Amy stopped. For a minute she just couldn't place who it was. Certainly she knew the voice. She knew she knew it, but…she turned.

Running towards her, arms outstretched, was a tall, pretty girl, who looked as if she might be sixteen or seventeen—though Amy knew she was only fourteen. She was dressed casually in jeans, sweater and trainers. Her long hair was tied back. And she looked delighted to see Amy.

Before Amy could move or say anything, she was enveloped in a great hug. 'I've missed you,' a voice against her shoulder said rapidly. 'How I've missed you, me and Dad both. It was rotten when you had to leave and we couldn't even say goodbye. Then we had to go to Canada and we're here now and I'm so glad we've found you, Amy. I need you, I need a friend.'

Amy hugged the girl back. 'It's good to see you, too, Johanne,' she managed to gasp. She felt numb, bewildered, unable to think, her mind grappling with what was happening. Johanne Ross was here. She said she and her dad had missed her. That meant…

Odd facts clicked together in her mind. The practice was short of a locum. She had heard that one who might be suitable was coming for interview. It could be…please, no… Not this, just when she'd got some kind of balance into her life. Please, not this.

Unsteadily, knowing that her voice was wobbling, she said, 'Is your…? Are you…?'

'Dad's got it! He was interviewed this morning, they are just doing what they call settling things and he's going to start practically at once. Amy, I'm so happy to be here with you.'

Johanne stepped back, releasing Amy. 'Look who's here—Dad!'

Somehow Amy managed to turn. A very familiar voice said, 'Hello, Amy.'

That deep voice! She remembered the first time she had heard it, remembered what it did—always did—to her. 'Hello, Adam,' she managed to say.

For a moment all feeling, all emotion deserted her. She wasn't aware of the receptionists' desk, the familiar surroundings. She couldn't hear the chatter from the adjoining room or smell the expensive floor polish. All her attention was focussed on the man in front of her.

And—for now—she felt detached, as if this was happening to someone else. How could it happen to her? She had intended never to see this man again.

She looked at him as if seeing him for the first time, checked his appearance, itemised everything that she could see, as if to convince herself that it was really him. He was dressed in well-polished black shoes, a perfectly cut dark suit, pure white shirt, college tie. His hair was as she remembered it, curly, unruly. It provided a touch of something different from the perfectly groomed rest of him. And his face…

Although she had desperately tried not to, she had

thought of his face so often. It came to her at night, when she was in that half awake, half asleep state. It came unexpectedly during the day at work, when she was faced with some apparently insoluble problem. Much to her annoyance, his face haunted her.

It wasn't a handsome face—rugged would be a better word. And if the grey eyes sometimes looked so icy that she felt one glance would freeze—well, that generous mouth always looked forgiving. And she knew it was so kissable.

That thought made her shudder. She had to get control of her emotions, deal with this situation.

Then she remembered the first time they had met, by the pool in Majorca. She remembered how he had affected her—an instant, out of time, when she had felt something that she had never expected to feel again. And that something had grown, so much…

Concentrate! Deal with this!

From somewhere she summoned a polite, a professional voice and said, 'Adam! I never expected to see you again. What are you doing here?'

She knew she hadn't fooled him, that he could sense her inner turmoil. But he said, equally formally, 'I'm part of the team now. I've been taken on here as locum for six months. I'm looking forward to working with you, Amy. We worked well together before. Remember? On the beach?'

She could tell that he was thinking far more than he was saying. And how well she did remember before—how could she ever forget it?

Her world had lurched out of kilter when she had first seen Johanne, only now was it coming back to normal. She began to comprehend that he was really, truly here. And he was going to work with her. She stared at him, this time with more caution. The first thing to find out was if he was angry with her. She supposed he was entitled to be. But at the time she had done the only thing she had felt she could, the thing that would be best for both of them.

She said, 'We did work well together, didn't we? And I supposed I enjoyed it in one way. We were supposed to be on holiday but doctors and nurses never truly stop working, do they? But why come here? Why did you want to...? How did you...?'

She became aware of Johanne, listening to this strained conversation and looking from one to the other with an alert eye. He became aware, too. He took keys out of his pocket, gave them to his daughter and said, 'Nip out to the car, Johanne, and pick up those photographs, I think they're on the back seat. I'm sure Amy would want to see them.'

'All right, I'll go,' said Johanne, making it obvious that she knew she was being dismissed, 'but I'll be right back.'

Adam waited until Johanne closed the door behind her and then came over and took Amy's shoulders in his hands. He said, 'I won't offer to shake hands with you, I think we're better friends than that.'

She felt her body go rigid as he bent over and kissed her gently on the cheek. That smell of citrus aftershave! There was a rush of memories, feelings, emotions and she wondered if and how she could cope. But she managed it somehow. He released her, stepped back and smiled.

'Do the...have you told the doctors that we know each other?' she managed to croak.

He nodded. 'It was no great secret. I told them that we met casually on holiday, that you got on very well with Johanne. You'd mentioned where you worked and that there might be a vacancy in a few weeks. So when I saw the advert I just applied.'

'I see. And is that the real reason you're here?'

'You know it's not.' He looked over her shoulder. 'Johanne's coming back. We don't want to talk in front of her, she's knowing enough already. Now, we're staying for a few nights at the Gilmour Arms. I can leave Johanne alone there tonight. Can we get together then? Perhaps I could take you to dinner?'

'Why do you want to take me to dinner?' Amy asked. She knew she was playing for time.

His voice took on that slightly harsh note that she had heard on occasion before, and she remembered that he was not a man to take lightly. 'Amy, we're going to be together for six months. There are things we just have to sort out. For a start, how we treat each other. I've made this happen and I know it could be hard on both of us. We need to talk. So can we have dinner together?'

'You forget, I have a young daughter, I can't just go out in the evening. Anyway, I'm not sure I want to talk—not yet anyway. You've known about this for, well, days. It's new to me and I'm still…still a bit shocked.'

'I can see that. But the sooner it is done, the better it will be.'

She knew he was right. They had to talk in private. 'I suppose so,' she said.

She frowned as she thought about what was possible. She knew her mother was out tonight so she

couldn't babysit. So there was no way she could leave
Elizabeth. And although she didn't want this meeting,
the best thing to do would be to get it over quickly.
There was only one answer. Hastily, she scratched her
address on a piece of paper. 'This is where I live. If
you want to come round—say, about eight—we could
have a coffee together. But you can't stay long. My
house is along the Buxton road. When you get—'

'I'll find it. I'll buy a map. If I'm coming to live
here, I'm going to need one, aren't I?'

She shivered. Buying a map brought it home, that
they would be working together. He would be finding
his way round her territory, probably visiting some of
her patients. But she merely said, 'Is eight all right
for you?'

'Perfect. There's a film on TV, which Johanne
wants to see. I don't. I'll be there.'

Johanne banged back into the room. 'No photos
there, Dad. You must have left them somewhere else.
I think you're losing it.'

'Comes with old age,' he said.

Johanne went on, 'So will we...?'

Behind them another door opened and one of the
two senior partners of the practice, Dr John Wright,
came in. He smiled at Amy and said, 'Things will be
easier for everyone now. I gather you've met Dr Ross
before. I'm pleased that you recommended us to him,
he's going to be a real asset to the practice.'

'It was his decision to come here,' Amy said. 'I
didn't really try to persuade him. Now, there are
things I must do.'

She turned and had to stop herself from running
into the practice staff room. She received several

cheerful greetings, and no one seemed to notice that her world had been turned upside down. Someone poured her a coffee and handed it to her.

'Met our new doctor yet?' asked Rita Jones, the receptionist. 'A bit dishy, isn't he? Daughter seems a nice girl. I wonder what his wife is like.'

Amy just couldn't go into it all just yet. 'I'm sure we'll find out,' she said.

Somehow she got through the rest of the day, doing the flu jabs for the over sixty-fives. She was kept busy, smiling, saying hello to the many familiar faces. There was always the danger that patients would think this was an opportunity for a chat so they had to be gently hurried on their way.

The work stopped her thinking, brooding over what had happened—and what might happen. She wondered fearfully if Adam might just drop in to see her at work—but he didn't. The work was simple and mechanical so there was no danger of making a mistake. But she was still happy when it was all over and she could get away a bit early.

She collected Elizabeth from her mother's house, had a quick cup of tea and a short chat. All she said about Adam arriving was that a new doctor was starting and that things might be a bit easier now. Then she drove home, Elizabeth strapped firmly in her car seat.

Heather Cottage was a perfect place for Amy and Elizabeth to live. Amy had been glad to move out of her previous house, which had been large, detached, on a pretentious estate on the outskirts of town. This suited the two of them much better.

It was a stone, end-of-terrace house, with a garage at the side. There was a small back garden, easy enough to keep tidy and somewhere for Elizabeth to play. Downstairs was a big sitting-room with an open-plan kitchen at the back, upstairs was a bathroom and three tiny bedrooms. It was cheap to run and heat, easy to keep clean. Just what Amy wanted and needed. She had got rid of nearly all the new furniture from her previous house. She hadn't liked it much anyway.

Now Adam was coming to visit and she wondered what he would make of it. It was certainly different from where they had first met.

Quickly out of her uniform and on with jeans and sweater. 'We're going to play now, Elizabeth, aren't we?'

'Bricks,' said Elizabeth joyfully. 'I want bricks.' So Amy shook out the box of wooden bricks with the letters on, and together they made walls and towers with words on them.

Amy loved her evenings playing with Elizabeth. All right, Elizabeth was her child, but she knew from experience of other people's children that Elizabeth was a good child. From her earliest days she had been easy to get to sleep. Now she smiled, laughed, was everybody's friend and was nearly always happy.

So they played, then had tea, then went up for a bath, bed and a story. Elizabeth fell asleep quickly. Amy kissed her daughter's cheek and went down-stairs. Happy time was over.

It was seven o'clock, and Adam would come in an hour. Amy tidied the room and then put on coffee to percolate, arranged biscuits on a plate. Or perhaps she should offer something different? She found a bottle of wine, fetched and polished two glasses. Then she looked at the label on the wine bottle. It was one that she had brought back from Spain, a vintage that they had drunk together. No, they couldn't drink that one. Too many memories. She fetched another bottle, a birthday gift from Dr Wright.

What was she doing? Why all this fuss? He had practically invited himself here, she hadn't wanted him to come. But perhaps she could hide behind the appearance of being an urbane hostess. It would make her feel more confident. Urbane hostess? Dressed like this in jeans and old sweater? Perhaps she should show herself as a working mother, clean but slightly scruffy.

She stood in thought a moment. Then she went upstairs, showered and then searched through her wardrobe for a dress. She didn't have much use for dresses—she didn't go out much. But she found a pretty blue one that would do.

She opened her underwear drawer. Her eyes passed rapidly over the lacy things in the back of the drawer—no, too many memories. She picked out a white bra and knickers, plain and sensible. Which was what she had to be, plain and sensible.

It didn't take long to dry her hair and put on a touch of make-up. Appearance checked in the mirror, yes, quite presentable. He would be here in fifteen minutes. She went back downstairs and took a glass of iced water from the fridge.

As she sat, she realised that since she had first seen Adam that afternoon, she had resolutely refused to think about him. She had found other things to occupy her mind—it was called displacement activity. But now she had to work out some kind of plan of action. She wondered what he would make of her. Then she wondered what she should make of herself.

Her thought drifted backwards. It was now mid-October. It had happened six or seven weeks ago. It seemed so close! Life before then had been grey, but tolerable. Then those few golden days and life after that had been… She would be honest with herself. Without him it had been hard.

CHAPTER TWO

IT HAD started in this very room. It had been a Saturday morning, her mother had called in and they had been having a coffee together. The post arrived, the usual collection of junk mail, letters to do with her being a district nurse, most easily discarded. And just one official-looking letter from her solicitor.

Amy had slit it open, read the letter and blinked. 'Ma! It's a cheque! Fifteen hundred pounds. Some late payment to Paul's estate from an insurance company.'

'Very nice,' said her mother. 'More than enough to have a really good holiday with.'

'Holiday? I don't need a holiday. I was thinking of a new kitchen in a year or two. Now I can—'

'Your present kitchen is fine and you do need a holiday. You're getting thinner every day, and getting irritated far too easily. You need a complete break for a couple of weeks and you need to be pampered. This has not been a good year for you.'

Amy was bewildered. 'But I just can't go… There are things I ought to do…'

'Like what?' her mother demanded. 'Amy, you're just making excuses.'

Amy tapped the side of her chair. 'People just don't go on holiday like that,' she said crossly. 'I'd have to…'

And then it happened. Her wedding ring slipped

off her finger. It had been loose for a while, she had lost so much weight. She bent to pick it up, but her mother was there first and grabbed it. 'It's a sign, Amy! Let go! Your husband is dead, you're not married any more. You even changed back to your maiden name.'

She held the ring in the air as Amy tried to snatch it from her, and went on, 'Look, you've always been honest with yourself. That man was never anything but evil. He looked gorgeous but he stole your money and hit you when he was drunk—which was most of the time.'

'Ma, he was my husband. And he's dead!'

'Dead? And whose fault was that? You finally told him you were going to divorce him. So what does he do? Gets drunk yet again, smashes his car into a wall and is carted off to hospital. They told you there that he was never going to recover consciousness again— he was in a persistent vegetative state. He didn't even have the decency to die. And for two years you visited him three times a week, though all feeling for him had gone!'

'He was still the man I married.'

'We all make mistakes. Yours was bigger than most. We both know that man was bad and would never have changed. Now, stop feeling sorry for yourself and say you'll go on holiday.' Her mother's tone softened. 'You need it Amy.'

'But I can't just… There's Elizabeth and—'

'Yes, you can just! Elizabeth would love to go on holiday! And look at you! You're thin, pale, got rings under your eyes. If ever a woman needed a break, you do.'

Amy didn't know what to say. Of course, it was quite impossible. It was a lovely idea but she would have to say no and…

Coaxingly, her mother said, 'Give me one good solid reason why you can't go on holiday and I promise not to say another word. Just one real reason.'

So she sat there, mind churning, not able quite to say what she felt. Because she didn't know what she felt. She just didn't want to be pushed, just wanted to be left alone in her own little world. But… 'When should I go? You know I'd have to clear things at the surgery…'

'Details,' her mother said with some satisfaction. 'We can work them out later. Now, this ring.'

She gave it back to Amy who fumbled, about to slip it back on her finger. Then her mother held up her hand. 'Amy, you're not married any more. And there's certainly no happy memories with that bit of jewellery. So drop it in there with the rest of the junk.' She pointed to a brass jar on the mantelshelf, full, as such jars were, with rubbish.

Amy paused, felt that she was making an important decision. Then she dropped in the wedding ring. There was a moment's silence. 'I feel better,' she said.

So she decided to go on holiday. Both her mother and the staff of the surgery thought it was a great idea. Dr Wright especially urged her to go. 'I've had my eye on you for a while, Amy,' he said. 'You're not at your best. I couldn't prescribe anything better than a fortnight in the sun.' And then she found she was rather looking forward to it.

Once her mother had got a firm decision from Amy

that she would go on holiday, she moved quickly to prevent her daughter from changing her mind. 'You haven't bought anything new for years. This is to be a luxury holiday in a luxury hotel. You need a few luxurious clothes.'

She took Amy to Manchester so they could buy a complete new wardrobe. 'Just a few clothes,' she said. 'And get some new make-up, it's time you changed your image.'

'Didn't know I had an image,' said Amy.

She had thought perhaps an item or two from a popular chain store. Her mother had different ideas and had marched Amy first to an expensive under-wear shop. 'We'll dress you from the inside out,' she said to Amy. 'Nothing like fancy undies for making a girl feel good. Get six pairs of those, in different colours.'

'They're not going to keep me very warm, are they?' Amy asked, blinking at the price. But she had bought them—and the shoes, T-shirts, shorts, bikini and three dresses for evening.

'Who am I supposed to impress?' she cried as they finally moved towards the accessories department.

'You're impressing yourself.' Her mother smiled. 'If you look good you'll feel good. And if you feel good you'll be better.'

It was a wonderful hotel, in Cala d'Or, on the south coast of Majorca. The travel agent had picked well, and at her mother's insistence he had found a place that offered a babysitting service. Amy had said it wasn't necessary, but her mother had said serenely that it was optional. Anyway, she was very happy.

She had a large bed in a large room, with the balcony overlooking the pool. Elizabeth was delighted with her smaller bed which had been placed at one side. Amy stood on the balcony, leaned out and smelled the scent of orange trees. 'We're going to enjoy ourselves here,' she told Elizabeth.

'Want to swim,' said her daughter.

It took a couple of days for her to settle down. She lay by the pool in her bikini, liberally smeared with sunscreen, a thick holiday romance in one hand, a long iced drink by her side. And suddenly she would jerk upright, as if it wasn't right, as if there were things to do.

Every morning Elizabeth went off for a while with the kiddie reps and played with other children. They had face-painting, swimming competitions, modelling. She was a happy child who made friends easily, and at times Amy wondered why she herself couldn't be as happy. But it was good to hear Elizabeth's shrieks of laughter.

She phoned her mother the first two nights. 'I'm fine, Lissom's fine, the practice is fine,' her mother said waspishly after the second call. 'If not, we'll let you know. Now, stop worrying and enjoy yourself.' So Amy stopped phoning.

And after two days she found that she could. She was beginning to realise just how tense she had been. And she was realising that this new calmness was what she needed.

Breakfast and lunch were buffet service, but in the evening dinner was more formal. They dined outside and Amy loved it. Most people made an effort to dress for the occasion, the women in cocktail dresses or something long, the men in lightweight suits. The place looked cosmopolitan, sophisticated.

There was one thing her mother had insisted on. 'Promise me you'll use the babysitting service. Or at least find out what it's like.' Amy had been doubtful, but had discovered that she could hire a middle-aged English woman to sit with Elizabeth. Mrs Gonzalez came from Birmingham but had married a Spaniard. Elizabeth took to her at once, and Amy felt comfortable leaving her child with her.

After dinner the guests would walk a few feet to the terrace by the side of the pool, sit at small tables and drink. There was a small dance floor there, sometimes a band played, sometimes there was dancing. On occasion she was asked to dance, usually by people she had talked to over breakfast or lunch. Always, Amy politely refused. She was here to sit, to take things easy.

On the fourth night something different happened. Amy felt tired, and thought that she would go for a last walk around the grounds before going to bed early.

There were a number of little paths curving through the hotel grounds. They were lit by foot-level lamps, there was the smell of flowers and the distant salt of the sea. Amy looked upwards and through the drooping fronds of a palm tree she could see stars that were brighter than any she had seen in England. She liked it here.

Near the edge of the sea was a smaller swimming pool. The lights by it were out, the gate leading to it closed and locked. After a certain time no one swam here as it was unsupervised.

There was no one nearby. Amy heard a splash. Someone was in the pool.

It wasn't her business. If someone chose to be foolish, they were entitled to. But Amy's work often dealt with people who had chosen to be foolish. It wouldn't hurt just to go and look.

Looking might not hurt but it wasn't easy. Somehow she had to negotiate the locked gate. By the time she had forced her way through the shrubbery around the pool she was not in a good temper.

Although there were no lights here, Amy could see that there was a girl or young woman wading into the pool. She saw a towel and a pile of clothes on a chair. The girl heard Amy approaching, turned and placed her hands on her hips. Amy recognised the body language. This was a girl, not a woman. And she was ready for an argument.

'It's a lovely evening,' Amy said, and sat on one of the chairs.

After a pause the girl said, in an aggressive voice, 'I suppose you're going to tell me that it's not allowed and unsafe to swim here on your own.'

Amy shook her head. 'No. You obviously know it already and it is your decision. Isn't it a lovely evening?'

There was no reply. After a while the girl waded farther into the water. Amy made herself relax, the best thing to do was say nothing. Then the girl said, 'I just got fed up with people in there. All that noise and shouting…I needed to get away.'

'Fair enough,' said Amy. 'When you say "fed up with people", do you mean people in general or just one or two?'

The girl considered this. She said, 'Just one, I suppose. My dad. We had a row, he left me in my room. I waited till he'd gone then came here for a swim. OK?' Her tone was truculent.

'It's nothing to do with me,' said Amy. 'I can't talk you out of something you really want to do. Where's your mum?'

'She left us,' the girl said. 'About three years ago.'

Amy picked up on the word 'us'. She thought it was important.

'Your dad,' she said, still in the same careless tones, 'does he love you?'

The girl was indignant. 'What kind of question is that? Of course he loves me…I suppose. He just doesn't understand me.'

Where have I heard that before? Amy thought, but said nothing. 'You know you could come to harm here,' she said conversationally. 'I'm a nurse, I remember working on A and E one night when a girl about your age was brought in, she'd been midnight bathing on her own.'

'And?'

'We thought she was DOA,' said Amy, equally laconically. 'That means dead on arrival. In fact, technically, she was dead. But we worked on her for half an hour and somehow we got a pulse and then she slowly came to. Her mother was waiting outside. I would have been the nurse who had to show her the body but instead I got to tell her that her daughter had survived, which was good. How would your dad feel if he had to identify your body?'

The girl stood perfectly still and the silence stretched on. Amy was determined not to break it. But she gave a silent sigh of relief when the girl walked out of the pool. She picked up a towel, wrapped it round herself and sat next to Amy.

'OK,' the girl said, 'you got what you wanted and I'm not sure how you did it. Will you tell me?'

Amy shrugged. 'I'm a district nurse,' she said. 'I go round to people's homes to meet them. It's not just dressings and injections, you know, you have to talk to people as well. You didn't want to risk your life. You wanted someone to talk to.'

'He just won't listen! Look at me! I'm…I'm…'

'You're about fourteen,' said Amy, 'but you feel much older. And I must say you look much older, too.'

The girl was obviously pleased at that. 'I'm thirteen,' she mumbled, 'but my birthday's quite soon.'

Amy nodded. 'Let me guess. He wouldn't let you go into town—or off on your own somewhere?'

'There's a couple of lads who work behind the bar. They said they were going to a night disco and did I want to come.'

'Older lads?'

'What do you think? Of course they were. Anyway, I said I was going to bed early. Dad was downstairs so I crept out of my room, thinking of taking a taxi into town. Then I realised that I had no money. But I had to do something so I came here for a swim.'

'Sometimes it's hard, being thirteen,' said Amy. 'I'm Amy Harrison, by the way. You are?'

'Johanne—Johanne Ross. Pleased to meet you.'

There was a slightly formal handshake and then Amy said, 'Well, Johanne, if you're going to swim I'll sit here and watch you. Or if you've calmed down, you can go back to your room. I told you I'm a district nurse, I see a lot of girls your age. You might think it hard, having an over-protective father. Believe me, it's worse having one who doesn't care at all.'

There was silence for a while, and Amy tried to remain apparently indifferent. 'Thanks for the talk. Guess I'll go back into my room,' said Johanne. Quickly, she dressed. 'I'll probably see you around. Good night, Amy.' And she was gone.

Amy sat there in the darkness. She hoped she had helped solve Johanne's problems, she remembered how hard life had seemed at that age. Then she wished it was as easy to solve her own problems. She went back to Elizabeth.

Next day she had booked a day out. She went with Elizabeth on a coach trip to the north shore and they thoroughly enjoyed themselves. They were back quite early, and Amy put Elizabeth to bed for an afternoon sleep. Her little girl had asked if she could stay up late, just once, to watch the dancing. 'Just once,' Amy had said. 'And I'll let you put my new chiffon scarf round your head.'

'Chiffon scarf!' said the delighted Elizabeth. 'I'm going to be beautiful!'

'You are beautiful, darling,' Amy said.

So they went down to dinner together and then they went out to sit by the pool. Elizabeth was entranced. She loved the lights, the band playing on the other side of the pool. Amy stroked her daughter's hair. It was good that they were happy together. Vaguely, she wondered if she'd see Johanne. She'd like to chat to the girl again.

She looked up to see a man approaching. He was walking carefully round the pool edge, looking apparently casually at the people sitting down, as if he was searching for someone but didn't want to be too obtrusive. He was a tall, broad-shouldered man, though because of the low lights round the pool his face was in shadow. Then it became obvious that he was approaching their table—not another man asking her to dance? But Amy was sure she hadn't noticed or spoken to him before. She would have remembered.

He came to their table, turned and looked at Amy. Amy shivered with apprehension. What did he want? As his face came into the light she felt a charge run through her body. It was a feeling she had known before—but not for years now. The knowledge that a man was interested in her as a woman. And then he saw her more clearly. He frowned, looked puzzled, and she knew that he was feeling the same. She shook herself, she was being silly.

He spoke, and she loved his voice. Deep, musical, with a caressing tone that made her feel instantly that this man was interested solely in her. She shook herself again. It was a voice, no more.

Cautiously, he asked, 'Excuse me, am I talking to Amy Harrison?'

'Yes, I'm Amy Harrison.' Where had he learned her name?

Then she found out. 'Ah, the district nurse. I'm Adam Ross, Dr Adam Ross. I'm Johanne's father. Do you think I might sit down a moment?'

Amy hesitated a moment and then said, 'Of course.'

He took a seat, looked at Elizabeth and said, still cautiously, 'May I ask if it's Mrs or Miss Harrison?'

Amy hesitated again. Then she said firmly, 'I'm Miss Harrison—now. I used to be Mrs Handing but now I'm not married and I went back to my maiden name. And this is my daughter Elizabeth—also Miss Harrison.'

'I'm very pleased to meet you both.' He shook hands with her, and then, solemnly, with Elizabeth. 'That's a very nice scarf you're wearing in your hair Elizabeth.'

'It's chiffon! And it's my mummy's.' Elizabeth was delighted.

'Miss Harrison, I think you know how grateful I should be to you. May I get you a drink? There's a Cava here that I very much like. And an orange juice for Elizabeth? With a bendy straw?'

'I want a bendy straw,' said Elizabeth.

For a moment Amy thought of saying no. Accept a drink from a total stranger? But she was on holiday, so why not? 'Thank you, I'd like that, and Elizabeth would love an orange with a bendy straw. Where's Johanne tonight?'

'She'll be with us in a moment. I said I wanted to speak to you first. In fact, she feels a bit…foolish I suppose.'

'No need, she's young. We were all young once.'

He winced. 'Was I like Johanne? Were you like Johanne? Please, don't answer, I don't like to think of it.'

He lifted his arm, a waiter moved over at once to take the order.

'Did you ask for a bendy straw?' Elizabeth demanded when the waiter had left.

'I asked. But we must wait and see, you might get a surprise. Ah, here's Johanne.'

Johanne looked a little nervous as she approached the table, sat in the seat that her father courteously pulled out for her. She smiled at Amy, cast a careful eye at her father as if wondering what had been already said.

Before there could be any more conversation the waiter returned with the first half of the order—the Cava had to be fetched from the cellars. There was a lemonade for Johanne, an orange for Elizabeth—with not one bendy straw, but two. There was also a little monkey figure, mounted on a spring and fastened to the edge of the glass. When Elizabeth picked up her glass the figure bounced and waved and rocked. She thought it wonderful. 'Look, Mummy, he's dancing! My monkey is dancing like all of those people there. I was dancing this morning with the Beach Babes!'

'My name is Johanne,' Johanne said to her. 'Would you like to dance here, with me?'

'Yes,' Elizabeth said after a moment's thought. 'Then I can come back and play with my monkey.'

Once again Johanne looked at her father. He said, 'If Miss Harrison doesn't mind, I think that would be a wonderful idea.'

'I think it's a wonderful idea, too,' said Amy.

'Come on, Beach Babe,' said Johanne, and led Elizabeth onto the dance floor.

'Since our families seem to be becoming friends,'

Amy said, 'perhaps we should do the same. Amy and Adam from now on?'

'Amy and Adam. I think that has a definite ring to it.'

He looked at her in silence as the waiter returned with the chilled bottle and the two champagne flutes, and poured the wine. The two of them lifted their glasses and sipped together, still without speaking.

Surprisingly, Amy didn't feel nervous. In fact, she was recognising feelings she hadn't known in years. This man was…attractive. She liked the way he walked, the way he looked, the courteous way he had introduced himself. She liked his voice, the slightly long hair, the craggy face. Then she shut down the feelings. She didn't ever want to experience that kind of thing again.

Adam said, 'Last night you talked to my daughter.' His voice hardened for a moment. 'She left her room—against my express wishes—and was about to do something stupid like go for a midnight bathe. She said that you talked to her. You didn't argue with her, force her to do anything she didn't want. You didn't even suggest. But because of you she came back.'

'How do you know all this?'

'I wouldn't have known, but she confessed this morning.' His expression changed, became half hurt, half perplexed. 'I didn't know what to say.'

'So have you got things sorted out between you?' Amy asked. 'She does love you, you know.'

He laughed. 'Sorted out? For the moment, yes. I love her, too, though at times she makes me very angry. It's hard, bringing her up. I suspect I'm not very good at it.'

'If you try, you can't go too far wrong,' Amy said.

'Perhaps not.' He shook his head, as if to shake away irritating thoughts. 'But I didn't come here to burden you with my problems. I came here to say thank you for helping Johanne. I really am most grateful.'

'I liked her, we got on. What I did was nothing.'

'It was a lot to me.' He turned to look at the dance floor. 'In spite of the age difference, our two children seem to be getting on.'

'Johanne seems good with her, and Elizabeth is a chatterbox. She'll talk to anyone—she's not shy like me. She loves music and dancing.'

Behind them the band stopped playing its rather cheerful, upbeat number. The bandleader smiled and acknowledged the applause—led by Elizabeth and, after a while, Johanne. Then he gave the signal for another, slower number. 'Would you like to dance, Amy?' Adam asked.

She hesitated—but just for a moment. A quick glance told her Elizabeth and Johanne were still engrossed. 'Yes, I would,' she said.

It was a slow dance. There weren't too many couples on the dance floor but enough so that the two of them didn't stand out. Adam was a good dancer, the firmness of his arm guided her well. She hadn't danced—really danced—with a man she felt attracted to for years now. And it didn't feel too bad.

Slowly, they circled the floor. There were open skies above, clear stars, the softness of a gentle breeze. It was romantic, she thought, and then laughed quietly to herself.

'I used to love dancing,' she said, 'though I've hardly done any recently. And you're very good.'

'I used to love it, too. But life gets in the way of what you really want to do.'

'You are telling me,' she said. Then they were silent for a while, and she was perfectly content.

They went back to their table. Elizabeth and Johanne were there now, roaring with laughter. Adam poured Amy and himself another glass of the sparkling white wine and ordered more orange and lemonade. And shortly after that it was time to take Elizabeth to bed. Amy could see that she was tiring.

'We're going on to Palma to look round tomorrow,' Johanne said, 'but will we see you tomorrow night? I've enjoyed being with Elizabeth.'

Amy shook her head. 'This was a special treat,' she said. 'Tomorrow Elizabeth has dinner in her room and goes to bed at the proper time.'

'Then will just you join us for dinner?' Adam asked. 'Meet for a drink first, at the bar, about eight o'clock?'

'I'd like that,' said Amy.

Next evening Amy found herself rather looking forward to meeting Adam and Johanne. She tried to persuade herself that it was Johanne that she was really interested in—but she knew it wasn't true.

She decided to wear a dress that so far had remained in the wardrobe. It was dark blue, and more than a little revealing. Amy looked at herself in the mirror, reminded herself that she mustn't bend forward. Then she put on her make-up—perhaps with more than usual care.

Johanne and Adam were waiting for her downstairs. Adam smiled, looked quietly pleased to see her. And Johanne beamed.

Adam was dressed much as he had been the evening before—in a dark linen suit, but this time with a white shirt instead of yesterday's pale green. Like nearly all the men there, he wore no tie. Amy thought he looked quietly elegant. Johanne, too, had obviously made an effort.

'I love your dress,' Johanne said to Amy. 'I wish I had one like that.'

Behind her, Amy saw Adam raise his eyebrows. He obviously thought—rightly—that this was not a young girl's dress. She managed to restrain a smile. 'I like your dress, too,' she said mildly to Johanne.

Johanne rolled her eyes. 'An evening dress? It's got sleeves! Guess who bought it for me.'

'Let's go through, shall we?' Amy said smoothly.

Amy enjoyed dinner. They talked about various safe things. Johanne asked if she could have wine, but when her father said that lemonade was better, she glowered a bit but accepted it with good grace. Amy could see that she was trying to behave well, to make a good impression. And at the end of the meal she said, 'Dad, Amy, I'm feeling a bit tired. D'you mind if I go to my room, watch a video? I'm falling asleep here.'

'Good idea,' Adam said. 'You've had a long day.'

So Johanne kissed Adam then, after a moment, Amy as well, and left. Adam and Amy looked at each other, suddenly thrown together. Amy guessed he was thinking the same as her. Where would the evening end? She didn't know herself.

Diffidently, he said, 'Dinner's over now. Shall we

get a table and a bottle, or would you like to walk a little?'

'I'd love a walk,' Amy said without hesitation. 'It's such a lovely evening. We've got an hour or so before I need to get back to Elizabeth.'

They set off down one of the little paths running between the pools, the changing cabins and the gardens. They met a few other couples walking along, hand in hand or arm in arm, and Amy wondered what she should do if he tried to hold her hand. She thought that she didn't want him to. But there was no problem, he didn't try. Was she disappointed?

Eventually they were on their own, on a rocky promontory. Silver light from the moon illuminated the sea. The sounds from the hotel were now distant. Below them was the hiss and gentle roar of the sea.

They sat on a convenient bench, some distance apart. 'I'm glad we can have some time on our own,' he said. 'I wanted to talk to you and this seems a good place for it.'

He stared around him and then said, his voice cynical, 'Romantic here, isn't it?'

She looked at him, rather disturbed. 'You don't sound romantic,' she said. 'But I know what you mean. And if you're interested, I share your feelings about romance. It's a con. Why did you want to talk to me?'

He didn't reply at once. She could tell he was having difficulty in beginning. 'The first reason is because I think you're a good listener. And you give good advice. What I heard about you from Johanne impressed me. I like you for what you did for her.

Then I met you—last night and tonight—and I was…I suppose…attracted to you.'

'I've heard more stirring declarations,' said Amy, 'but go on.'

He shrugged. 'That's as far as it goes. Now I think it's your turn. Tell me what you think. Do you really know? I don't think I do.'

Tell him what she thought. That was hard. Cautiously, she said, 'Neither of us can judge each other, we've barely spent half a dozen hours together. But what I've seen of you I guess I like. But I've been married. I made a big mistake and I don't want the bother of another man.'

He laughed. 'Another stirring declaration.'

There was silence for a while, but she felt it was a companionable silence. Then he said, 'I get the feeling that we are two wounded people. We're wary of what other people call romance. Sometimes, when you talk, you have a hunted look—as if you're not sure that other people mean you well. I'd like to know why. D'you want to tell me your story?'

She considered this. 'Not much,' she said. 'It's boring. Other people's troubles always are. And I'm not going to feel sorry for myself by going over it again. Anyway, why are you wounded?'

'Also boring,' he said after a while.

There was a pause, both of them looked out to sea. He moved his hand. She wondered if he would try to hold hers but, slightly to her disappointment, he didn't. Instead he took a coin from his pocket, spun it in the air and caught and covered it on the back of his hand. 'We'll bore each other,' he said. 'Heads or tails. If you get it wrong you go first. OK?'

It didn't take her long to decide. 'OK...I choose heads.'

He lifted his hand. The coin showed tails.

She couldn't speak at first. After a moment he said, his voice kind, 'If you feel you're not up to it, that is fine. Just do what you feel. But I really would like to know about you.'

Another pause. Then she said, 'Right, I'll tell you.'

CHAPTER THREE

SHE'D never told anyone the full story. A lot of her friends knew part or all of it—but this was the first time she had ever gone over it from start to finish.

'My name's Amy Elizabeth Harrison and I'm twenty-eight years old. I'm a district nurse in Lissom, which is a small town in Derbyshire. I love the place and I love my work. I have a daughter Elizabeth whom I dote on. I manage to bring her up and work because my mother happily helps out.'

She took a breath. That was the barest of outlines. Now came the hard part.

'I married a man called Paul Harding. His nickname was Golden Boy because he had this lovely blond hair, and on my wedding day I was so happy I was delirious. But…it didn't work out. He turned out not to be the man I thought I was marrying. But we kept up appearances, pretended to be happy. I suppose I had my pride. We had a new house full of new furniture and people thought we were a golden couple. But people just didn't know what he was like!'

She knew that her voice was rising, the emotion that she tried to keep suppressed was breaking through. She paused, and he reached out a hand and stroked her back. 'Nice and easy,' he said. 'There's no hurry.'

She found it helped, she could go on. 'After three years' misery I'd had enough. I had a one-year-old daughter by this time. So I told him that I was going to divorce him. I'd given all I had, made all the allowances I could, I just couldn't take any more. That was two years ago. He celebrated it by getting very drunk and nearly killing someone in a road accident. But he also nearly killed himself. Not quite, though. It was a pity really.'

That disturbed Adam. He looked at her, obviously surprised. 'I wouldn't have thought you were a bitter, vengeful person,' he said.

'You don't understand. He didn't die, but he wasn't living either. His body was alive but his brain was dead—a persistent vegetative state, they call it. No hope ever of a recovery. For two years he lay unconscious and I visited him three times a week—I don't know why. Then three months ago he died.' She gave a sad smile. 'If that's what love, romance is, keep me away from it. I'll never trust another man as long as I live.'

He nodded, leaned over to take her hand and squeeze it. Then, quickly, he let go. But she had liked the momentary contact, felt her heart lurch at his warmth. She waited a moment. 'Now it's your turn,' she said. 'First of all, where do you work?'

'At the moment I don't. I am—or was—a GP and I love the work. I was a partner in a practice near Bristol, happily married to a gorgeous girl, the daughter of a local rich farmer. We had baby Johanne practically at once. My wife was supposed to be some kind of a vet's assistant, but she did very little. Like you, I thought we were happy. Then things soured. She got bored with married life in the country. I had an offer to go to America to train to be a hospital doctor. She couldn't understand why I didn't take it up.'

'How were things between her and Johanne? Wasn't she happy to be a mother?'

He shrugged. 'Johanne was a toy for her. She alternated between not being able to do enough for her baby and leaving all the care to some nanny she'd employed. Perhaps that's why Johanne is so mixed up now. And she certainly didn't want any more children, though I did. Anything…physical between us soon disappeared.'

'Do you think any of this was your fault?'

He grinned at her. 'Don't mind asking awkward questions, do you? Well, yes, I suppose it was. I was working very hard and I thought that things would sort themselves out. I now realise that I missed out an awful lot on Johanne's early years. We saw too little of each other and sometimes I now think of the good times I could have had with her—and I didn't.'

'I know how doctors work,' Amy said feelingly. 'The good ones often try to do too much. But what happened then?'

'After a time things did get easier, she seemed more content. Only later did I find out that she was seeing an older, much richer man.'

'Been in that situation,' said Amy. 'Not nice, is it?'

'Not nice at all. But in time she persuaded him to marry her, and told me she wanted a divorce. However, he didn't want someone else's daughter. I was very happy with this. I negotiated a settlement that gave me complete custody of Johanne. And I'm doing my very best to give her what her mother never did.'

Amy was horrified at what she had just heard. She thought of Elizabeth, her feelings for her daughter. How could anyone give away their own child? Then she thought of what Adam had said last. 'You're trying to give Johanne what her mother never did?' she said. 'What exactly is that?'

'Well, love,' he said. 'And certainty. It sounds so simple, but it's not. I'm not sure I'm doing the right things. But nothing will stop me trying. Most of the time she's fine. Just occasionally she seems to get things wrong—and then we fight.'

Amy wondered if this was the right attitude, but decided to say nothing. She felt so much for this honest but troubled man. He deserved better!

He went on. 'I've given up the practice and we're having this holiday. It's supposed to bring us together, but so far that hasn't been tremendously successful. Then we're going to Canada, to my brother's for a few weeks. And then…who knows?'

There was silence. Eventually, she said, 'We're both in a mess, aren't we?'

'Two troubled souls. But talking to you has made things a bit easier. What do we do now?'

She thought. What *did* they do now? 'I don't know,' she said. 'I'm scared and you're scared.'

'True.' He said nothing for a moment and then waved his arm, encompassing the sky, the sea, the semi-tropical gardens around them. 'This all doesn't seem true. It's a holiday, things happen that don't happen in hard real life. Would you have told your story to a stranger if you had met him in Lissom?'

'No. But now you don't seem a stranger.'

'Nor do you. Amy, we're here for a fortnight. Four

days have gone, ten to go and things are different here. Let's see quite a bit of each other. Probably mostly with Johanne and Elizabeth, of course. We'll not behave like young lunatics, this won't be that kind of holiday romance. But we'll see something of each other. OK?'

'Of course,' she said. Then, not sure of where the impulse came from, she leaned over and kissed him on the cheek. 'Now we'd better get back,' she said.

The four of them met at breakfast next day. Adam had hired a car and invited Amy and Elizabeth to go with Johanne and him across the island, where there was a popular beach he had been told about. Amy thought that would be a safe and pleasant way of spending time with him.

Elizabeth had always been a friendly child. She took to Johanne at once—perhaps because Johanne wanted to play with her. Amy had wondered about how she would take to Adam—she didn't see too many men. But Adam appeared instantly smitten with Elizabeth. When he was sure she wouldn't mind, he lifted her over his head, told her she was a flying little girl and asked her to wave her arms. Elizabeth loved this, and adored Adam at once.

Adam had gone to some trouble that morning to buy a cassette of stories for four-year-olds in English. He played one as soon as they all got into the car. Elizabeth was entranced by this, especially as two of the stories she knew already. She'd never heard a story played on the car radio before. Amy thought it was a brilliant idea, and decided to buy a selection when she got back home. She also thought that it showed what a thoughtful man Adam was.

The sun beat down on them. In between leaving the air-conditioned car and reaching the beach, they had all got hot and sticky. There were rocks handy; they disappeared behind them to get changed.

'Look at this,' said Johanne as they reappeared. She was wearing a thick, rather unflattering costume. 'It looks horrible. This is a school uniform for going into the water. I wanted to buy a bikini but Dad said, no, I was too young. And you look gorgeous.'

'I'll have a word with your dad,' said Amy, 'but it is really his choice.'

In fact, she was feeling rather shy. The bikini that had seemed fine in the shop suddenly looked very revealing. So far, Adam hadn't seen her in a swimsuit. She wondered what he would think.

Adam was already in the water. The three of them ran down to the edge of the sea to where he was waiting for them, the sea washing round his thighs. Amy could hardly take her eyes off him. He looked great in swimming shorts and the muscles hinted at by his usual clothes were revealed. She felt herself going warm. Not an ounce of fat, he had the body of a Greek god.

Embarrassed by her thoughts, Amy turned to her daughter. She didn't want to think about his body.

Elizabeth was already quite a competent swimmer, but had only ever swum in swimming pools. The vastness of the sea—and the waves—both excited and scared her, so for a while she had all Amy's attention. She heard a splashing behind her, felt the vibrations through the water, and Adam swam effortlessly past her. She was a good swimmer, but he was excellent.

After a while he swam over to her and said to Elizabeth, 'Would you like to come for a ride on a big fish?'

'Yes!' shouted Elizabeth. 'Big fish! Big fish! Where's the big fish?'

'I'm a big fish and I'm going to take you for a ride. Now, get on my back and put your arms round my neck.'

Elizabeth did as she was told. 'She'll be quite safe,' Adam whispered to Amy, and set off, now swimming a sedate breast-stroke. Elizabeth was delighted. 'Faster, big fish,' she shouted. 'Faster.' Adam did his best to oblige.

Elizabeth didn't want to get off her big fish. But after ten minutes Amy thought that Adam should be given the chance to swim on his own, and firmly collected Elizabeth. She noticed that Adam seemed as reluctant to stop as Elizabeth.

They swam for perhaps an hour. She noticed that Adam kept a careful eye on all three of them. When they felt they'd had enough, they walked back up the beach, found an open-air shower and rinsed the salt off their bodies. Amy towelled her hair dry as best she could then tied it up in a scarf. It might not look elegant, but who cared?

Twenty minutes' drive away they found a seaside town and managed to park in the shade of a giant tree. Good, the car would stay cool. Then they found an open-air café, ordered drinks and a seafood platter each. Swimming had given them an appetite.

After a while, Amy said, amiably but directly, 'Adam, I think you're being cruel to your daughter.'

He looked at her, astonished. 'What?'

'That bathing costume you're making her wear. It might be fine for the municipal baths in Sludgethorpe in 1955, but here she needs a two-piece.'

He laughed. 'Is that your own opinion, or was there some prompting?'

'Johanne did admire my costume,' Amy said with an air of injured dignity, 'but I couldn't admire hers.'

'But she's only a schoolgirl!' Adam wasn't convinced.

'She's a schoolgirl now,' Amy said, 'but in two or three years she'll be a young lady. And you need practice to be one of those, it doesn't come automatically. Buying a two-piece bathing costume isn't much of a declaration, Adam.'

'Please, Dad!'

'It appears that I'm outvoted,' he said dryly. 'All right, you can have a two-piece, but I'll come along to see that—'

'Let's all go,' said Amy, 'and make sure she buys something both nice and suitable.'

He sighed. 'Three ladies and me. I'm outvoted.'

They went to a nearby shop and bought quite a becoming bikini without too much trouble. And Adam insisted on buying Elizabeth a new sun hat, which delighted her. But then Elizabeth yawned and Amy looked at her daughter with concern. Elizabeth was tired, she needed to sleep.

'I'll go back to the car and Elizabeth can sleep there,' she said to Adam and Johanne. 'You two go for a wander round, we'll be perfectly all right.'

'I'll stay with Elizabeth if you like,' Johanne offered. 'I'm a bit tired myself and I've got a book with me.'

Adam and Amy looked at each other. 'I think that's a good idea,' Adam said eventually, 'I fancy a walk along the beachfront for a few minutes. Amy?'

'I'd like that, too,' she said.

Ten minutes later Elizabeth and Johanne were settled in the car and Amy and Adam set off for their walk. The street was busy but Amy felt as if they were in their own little shell, that only the two of them mattered.

'I like being with you,' he said. 'I feel I'm getting to know you. And though I like Elizabeth very much and I love my daughter, I like being alone with you. How do you feel?'

She thought for a moment. 'Scared,' she said. 'Not of you but of me.'

He nodded. 'I know what you mean. I feel a bit the same way myself. Now, would you like a drink or shall we walk a little more?'

'Let's walk,' she said.

They strolled along the front, passing thronged holidaymakers, shops on one side of the road and the harbour, with yachts moored, on the other. The sun was high and the sea and the sky burned with an impossible brightness.

'You're squinting. Your eyes must hurt,' he said. 'I'll get you a hat with a brim.'

'No, it's just that I forgot my sunglasses. I'll buy a spare pair.'

'I don't want you to wear sunglasses. I want to be

able to see your eyes. And if it will make you as happy as a hat made Elizabeth, then that'll be great.'

He took her arm, pulled her towards a shop. 'That hat there would really suit you.'

It was straw coloured, with a broad brim and a pretty ribbon that matched her dress. He took it down, put it on her head and then pointed her at a mirror. 'You're right. It does suit me,' she said. 'I really like it.'

Before she could object he had paid for it. 'Now you won't have to squint when you look at me. And I can see your eyes.'

'I usually buy my own clothes,' she told him.

'I just wanted to buy you something. It pleased me.'

'That's nice,' she said.

They walked farther along the front and after a while he took her hand. She liked it. No one but her daughter had held her hand in years.

They walked to the end of the road. It was quieter here, they leaned over the railing looking at the large bay, the high cliffs opposite.

'You haven't said anything for five minutes,' he told her, 'and I can't make out what kind of mood you're in.'

She looked down at his hand holding hers. 'I'm wondering what I'm getting into,' she said.

'You're getting into nothing. This is a holiday, a time away from ordinary life. We make the most of it.'

She lifted her head to look at him directly, not completely sure of what he meant. Solemnly, he looked back at her. She faltered, 'I'm not sure...'

Then she looked along the road behind him, saw two figures moving purposefully towards them. 'There's Johanne and Elizabeth,' she said. 'They seem rested.'

He turned to look. 'So they do,' he said casually. 'Yet another interrupted conversation. I suppose I'd better let go of your hand.'

'It might be better,' she said.

Things were just as relaxed the next day. Johanne chattered to Amy and played with Elizabeth—the two of them were getting on famously. Adam asked if he might be excused if he didn't join in the conversation too much, they were driving through the mountains and he needed to concentrate. Amy told him that she'd looked at the unguarded precipice at the side of the road and, as far as she was concerned, he could keep absolutely quiet. Everyone laughed.

Then they were on a flatter road and they put on Elizabeth's story tape again. The story they were listening to involved a big, big, big, bad, bad, bad giant. It was necessary to shout out 'big, big, big, bad, bad, bad' at frequent intervals. Elizabeth couldn't laugh enough—especially when Adam joined in with the deepest of voices.

Eventually they reached their destination. This was a different kind of beach. They were in a cove, with waves beating heavily on rocks at each side. The area where it was safe to swim was marked off by a set of yellow buoys, and there were notices in several languages telling them of the dangers. There weren't as many people here. Amy felt she rather preferred it.

Johanne rather shyly put on her bikini for the first

time, and was pleased when her father took out a camera and said he wanted a picture of her. Then the four ran down to the water and swam.

Yes, things were better. When she was swimming near him, Amy felt Adam's hand trail down her side. It could have been an accident—but perhaps not. Whatever it was, she liked it.

After a while three of them went back to sunbathe on the beach. Johanne said she wanted to stay in a little longer. Amy had noticed that she was nearly as good a swimmer as her father. Adam nodded to his daughter, told her to remember to stay inside the yellow buoys.

Amy dried and dressed Elizabeth then stretched out on her towel. Adam offered to walk up the beach and fetch them all an iced drink. 'Will you keep an eye on Johanne?' he asked Amy. 'I don't expect any trouble. She's sensible about swimming.'

'I think she's sensible about most things,' Amy said, and felt rather upset when he winced. But she watched Johanne swim as she slathered sunblock on her own now dry body.

Johanne was keeping well inside the yellow buoys. There were a few other swimmers, one or two weren't as disciplined. But Johanne was Amy's sole responsibility.

The sun shone high in the sky, reflecting off the water, at times making it difficult to see. Amy squinted a little, and then reached for her sunglasses—remembered today. But Johanne was still clearly visible.

Suddenly Amy saw her wave frantically, then point

to something by the rocks. A split second later Amy heard her scream for help.

But it wasn't Johanne who was in danger. Amy looked where she had pointed, saw a little scrap of red being tossed by the waves dangerously close to the rocks. It was a swimmer—apparently unconscious.

Amy turned, desperately waved both arms at the distant figure of the returning Adam. When she had his attention she pointed out to sea. Adam saw what was happening at once. He dropped the drinks he was carrying and ran for the water.

Amy tucked Elizabeth under her arm and, as quickly as she could, walked down to the beach. She could see that Johanne was swimming towards the figure, beyond the yellow buoys. Adam, now racing through the water, shouted, 'Johanne! Stop there now! I said stop!' Amy was pleased to see that Johanne obeyed as she was now dangerously near the rocks.

Adam was now swimming, a machine-like crawl that ate up the distance. He passed between the yellow buoys, passed Johanne. Now he, too, was in danger, and Amy saw him picked up by a giant wave, heaved high into the air. But he was near the figure, floating still in the water.

Another wave grabbed Adam and exploded against the rocks in white spray. Amy moaned. She thought he had been dashed against a rock. But then she saw him, still swimming, apparently with the unconscious swimmer in tow. He was moving much more slowly now.

Johanne had obeyed him when he had told her to stop swimming, but she was waiting outside the buoys. When her father came near her she grabbed hold of the figure and helped him pull it towards the beach. By now the water's edge was crowded with anxious onlookers who ran into the sea to help the couple pull the figure ashore. Elizabeth had sensed the mood and was crying.

It was a young girl—perhaps Johanne's age—in a red costume. Her limbs flopped lifelessly as she was lowered onto the sand.

Adam took charge at once. He rolled the girl over and water ran out of her mouth.

For a moment Amy didn't know what to do. She saw blood running down Adam's arm and a long gash across his back. But he wasn't in immediate danger, the girl probably was. Amy was a nurse, who'd worked for years in A and E. This kind of thing was her speciality.

By now a crowd had gathered, pushing dangerously close. Perhaps they wanted to help but they were doing the opposite. Amy pulled Johanne away and handed Elizabeth to her. 'Hold her and don't let her go. Get these people at least six feet away—we need space. Find someone with a mobile phone and send for an ambulance. Make sure that they know that the girl is unconscious, is not breathing so the call is prioritised. Check that it's done.'

'Right,' said Johanne.

Resuscitation room or Spanish beach, the techniques were still the same. ABC—airway, breathing, circulation. The first, all-important things to check.

Adam had checked that the girl had not swallowed her tongue. He said, 'Airway's patent but there's no breathing, no pulse.'

Vaguely Amy was aware of the crowd moving back. She could hear someone shouting at them like a sergeant major. Johanne must have passed on the message to someone more adult. In fact, Amy was aware of a frightened Johanne clutching Elizabeth and staring down at the lifeless body. Concentrate on what was important!

'Amy, you do mouth to mouth while I massage the heart.' He was the doctor, it was his decision to make.

Amy nodded and she knelt by the girl's head, held it by skull and jaw and eased it backwards so the airway was open. Ideally she should use a mask. Conditions here weren't ideal.

First she breathed into the girl, managed to get the chest to rise. Only then did Adam place his hands together over the heart, lean forward, stiff-armed, and start the rhythmic pressure that would force the blood to circulate.

Amy kept her lips pressed to the girl's cold mouth and blew air into her lungs. At least, there was no obstruction. So, in tandem and in rhythm, they worked together.

The two breaths, then fifteen compressions.

Amy managed to glance at Adam. He was completely absorbed, thinking only of what he was doing. There was blood running down his arm, dripping off his back, mingling with the seawater and the sweat. Amy looked at Johanne and said calmly, 'Tear up a couple of towels and see if you can put a rough dressing on those cuts on your dad's shoulder and back. But don't disturb his work and keep hold of Elizabeth.'

Adam looked up, nodded at Johanne. Johanne

stood there a moment, horrified. Then she did as she was told.

Amy and Adam worked on. Amy knew he wasn't conscious of the crowd, or even her. All his attention was on the lifeless figure between them. Did she have any chance of survival?

It was almost as if he read her thoughts. He looked up, sadly shook his head at her. Was there any point in carrying on? From behind them came Johanne's despairing voice. She had seen and realised the meaning of the signal between them. She cried, 'Dad, you can't give up now!' So they carried on desperately trying to maintain life until the ambulance arrived with a defibrillator.

And then, finally, they heard the ambulance siren.

CHAPTER FOUR

IT WAS good to be surrounded by a trained team, with all the equipment they needed. Within minutes, to everyone's relief, the paramedics had the girl's heart beating again and then lifted onto a stretcher and carried up the beach to the waiting ambulance. A paramedic made a lightning assessment of Adam's injuries and decided they weren't serious. He slapped field dressings on them and said that Adam should come to the hospital, too.

Adam shook his head. 'I'm a doctor, I can manage. As soon as I return to my hotel, I'll send for the doctor there.' The paramedic decided not to argue.

Now the crowd was drifting away. Amy and Johanne stood by their little pile of belongings, feeling a certain sense of anticlimax. Amy held Elizabeth close to her.

'Dad, I hate this beach,' Johanne said tearfully. 'I want to go home now. That girl nearly died!'

'I know,' said Adam, 'but she'll be alright now and you were such a great help, taking care of Elizabeth while Amy tended the girl.'

Amy hugged Johanne in agreement, then looked at Adam, now slightly pale. 'You'll be going into shock if you're not careful,' she said. 'I'll drive back to the hotel, we'll all be better there.'

'Good idea,' he said. 'Incidentally, if I ever want an emergency nurse I'll know where to look.'

'I'm a district nurse now. I much prefer it. Shall we go to the car?'

Adam didn't go into shock, he seemed much better on the drive home. He sat in the back, held Johanne's hand. Johanne sobbed quietly. Amy realised that this was perhaps her first meeting with near-death. And the girl had been about her age. It would put Johanne in mind of her own mortality. Elizabeth slept between them.

It was only early afternoon when they got back to the hotel. They parted in the lobby, Adam saying that a subdued Johanne needed a rest. Amy went to her room and showered, and then discovered that there was a Beach Babes meeting if Elizabeth wanted to attend. Elizabeth did want. The events of the previous few hours had passed her by.

Amy took her book to read on the balcony but just couldn't settle, so after half an hour she phoned Adam. Perhaps he wouldn't want to be on his own.

'Did you phone the doctor, Adam? What did he say about your cuts?'

His voice sounded weary. 'I didn't bother with the doctor. All I've got are superficial cuts and bruises.'

'A doctor who diagnoses himself has got a fool for a patient. How's Johanne?'

'She'll be fine. In fact, she's sleeping. I don't really approve, but I gave her a sedative. She'll be a lot better by dinnertime. Are you OK?'

'I'm fine. I did nothing.' She hesitated a moment and then said, 'I think I ought to come up to your room and have a look at you. I could borrow a first-aid kit from the hotel. After all, there's no way you can deal with a cut on your own back.' Then she paused and said, 'If you want me, that is.'

'I do want you. And I've seen you at work, you're a good nurse.'

Amy took a deep breath. 'So I'm coming. You're in room 704?'

'I am. Johanne's next door, we have connecting rooms.'

'So I'll be chaperoned?' Amy knew it was a feeble joke.

'Not really. Like all teenagers, Johanne can sleep through anything. Anything resembling work, that is.'

'Ten minutes,' said Amy.

She looked down at the outfit she had changed into. T-shirt and shorts. Not exactly a doctor's outfit, but she wasn't going to risk one of her new dresses. She went to Reception to borrow a first-aid kit.

Feeling a bit nervous, she tapped on his door. She got a shock when he opened it. He was clad only in a pair of shorts. Well, why not? And she had seen him dressed much the same on the beach. But somehow, here, his semi-nakedness was more obvious. As a nurse she was accustomed to walking into people's bedrooms, seeing them half naked, seeing evidence of their everyday, intimate lives. But here it seemed more personal.

There was a towel wrapped around his hand and she saw the temporary dressing on his shoulder was wet. He saw her looking and explained, 'I just had to have a shower. And I suppose everything got wet. But come in.'

'Your room is bigger than ours,' she said, just for something to say.

'It's the end of the row, on the corner. I've got a very secluded balcony—no one can see into it.'

'That's nice,' she said, going rather warm at the thought of Adam and herself hidden away together. 'And Johanne is…?'

He nodded at a door. 'Through there in her own room. She's sound asleep. Nothing will disturb her.'

'Good. Now, d'you want to sit by this table? I can see that your hand and your shoulder are hurt, and I remember there was a long gash on your back.'

'Jut minor,' he said. 'In A and E they wouldn't even merit the attention of a doctor.'

She stood up for her profession. 'In A and E they would be better dressed by a nurse than if a doctor did it.' Then she blushed as she saw him look at her, he had been teasing her.

She put the first-aid box on the table, opened it. The first thing she saw was a big packet of rubber gloves. It was second nature to put them on but here it didn't seem…well, friendly.

He saw her hesitation, grinned again. 'I do expect you to follow protocol, Nurse,' he said. So she snapped them on.

She was a nurse. For the moment this man was a patient. But it was hard to concentrate on work when the warmth of his body, the electric touch of his skin, the clean smell of soap and shampoo… Stupid thoughts! She had to get a grip.

He had injured his hand, his shoulder, his back. She recollected the wave that had tossed him against the rocks, he had been lucky. The hand and the shoulder were easily treated, she bathed and cleaned them and then put on fresh antiseptic dressings. The back was another matter. A jagged gash ran across from the right shoulder blade to just above the left kidney. She wondered if he knew how serious it was, he couldn't easily see it.

'We'll go into the bathroom,' she said. 'I want to do a better job of cleaning this.'

She washed the wound with antiseptic again, then examined it carefully—she had to ease out a couple of grains of sand. It must have hurt. She felt his muscles clench once or twice, then saw the deliberate attempt he made to relax. When she had finished she dabbed the wound dry, then sprinkled it with antiseptic powder.

'You're going to have to be careful how you move for a day or two,' she said. 'Ideally this should be sutured—but I'll close it with a set of butterfly stitches and that should do.'

When she had finished she covered the gash with a loose dressing, held on with sticky plaster. 'There, Adam, all done. I think you'll live.'

'And I think you're an excellent nurse.'

He watched as she repacked the first-aid box, and she found his gaze rather unnerving. After a while he pointed to a cupboard and said, 'I always take a small travelling kettle with me and a packet of tea. Would you like a cup?'

'That would be lovely. But I'm going to make it.'

She took his hand, felt for his pulse. 'Hmm. Still a bit fast. You must be a bit shocked still, you'd better sit down and rest for a while. Did it hurt when you hit the rock? In fact, does it hurt now?'

He thought about this. 'It didn't hurt when I hit the

rock, only afterwards. And it does…sting just a bit now. I can cope.'

'A typical male response. I suppose it's no good suggesting you lie on the bed?' Then she blushed when she saw his smile and realised what it had implied.

He said, 'Not really. But I'll go and lie on a lounger on the balcony. If you join me.' He saw her blush again and added, 'That's where Johanne and I relax.'

'I'll bring the tea through,' she said, trying to sound efficient.

While he carefully lay down on the lounger, she busied herself making the tea to stop herself thinking. Then she carried the tray out.

There were two loungers on the balcony, side by side. They had been pulled into the shade because of the heat of the afternoon. No one could see onto the balcony.

She handed him his tea, sat on the lounger next to him and drank her own. Neither of them felt the need to speak, and she realised that she was tired. He was probably more tired. When she had finished the tea, she gingerly lowered herself onto the pillow. It had been a hard half-day and, yes, she was tired. Just ten minutes' relaxation and she would… Her last thought was that it had been ages since she had slept with a man so close to her.

Amy wasn't sure what had wakened her. Something nice, she thought. She came awake slowly, not sure where she was, then remembered and felt quite happy to lie there with her eyes closed. Perhaps she was half-awake.

Something was touching her cheek. It tickled but it was pleasant. It wasn't a fly or anything like that and it moved gently down her cheek. When it reached the corner of her mouth she took it between her lips, touched it with her tongue, even bit it slightly. She recognised what it was. It was a finger.

A finger, stroking her cheek. Now, that was really nice. Then she came to full consciousness and jerked her head away. She opened her eyes fully—and there he was, looking at her, their heads not twelve inches apart. It was an intimacy that rather shook her.

'You look peaceful when you're asleep,' he said, 'you look happier, too.'

As he smiled down at her, Amy's first instinct was to sit upright. Then she decided that she didn't really want to. It was pleasant lying here in the warmth, with the smell of the sea and a nearly naked man next to her.

A what? A nearly naked man? That thought had crept up on her.

She rolled onto her side to face him. He did the same—but her nurse's eye noticed that he did it very cautiously. Now they were facing each other. She could feel the warmth of his breath, see his eyes very close to hers. They were grey, she noticed. And sometimes they changed in shade. Now they were darker, as if something had upset him—or excited him. His gaze seemed more intent.

His hand stretched out again, this time to her shoulder. It was the gentlest of touches, but she felt as if it burned her. And still he looked at her. She knew what he was thinking, knew what he was going to do, but there was nothing she could do about it. Nothing she wanted to do about it.

For a moment her body tensed, and she knew he could feel her anxiety. But then she sighed and her body relaxed. She fell onto her back again and closed her eyes. This wasn't the time to think, to worry. What would be, would be. And after all, she was on holiday.

His finger traced down her arm to caress the inside of her elbow, then to feel the thudding of the pulse on her wrist. Then it stroked upwards again, across her shoulder, and she caught her breath as it dipped inside the neck of her T-shirt. But it was only to run along the length of her collar-bone, then back across her neck to her cheek again, touching her lips. This time she deliberately caught his finger in her mouth, gave it the tenderest of bites.

She heard the creak of his lounger, felt his body move, and the light shining through her closed lids was suddenly darkened. He was leaning over her, poised on top of her. If she wanted, this was the time to stop him. But she didn't want. She felt as if a power other than herself was moving her. Her old life was discarded, there were no memories, there was only now.

His lips touched hers. She could tell by his gentleness that he didn't want to frighten her. Still the lightest of touches, still every chance for her to stop him. She didn't want to stop him. And his lips moved from her lips to her cheeks and then her closed eyes. She didn't want him to stop.

To her side she could feel his arm taking his weight as he leaned over her. She ran her hand up his arm, slid it round his back. She could feel the thickness of the dressing she had put on his back, she would have to be careful. And carefully she pulled him down towards her.

He kissed her lips again, but this time there was a difference. The kiss deepened and she moaned as his tongue probed, tasting her sweetness, bringing a sweetness of its own.

Somewhere in the back of her mind a shadow of doubt flickered. Was this a good idea? It certainly seemed a good idea. And her eyes remained shut. If she wasn't looking then she wasn't responsible.

Still with her eyes closed, she wriggled, rolled onto her side again, eased him across so the pair of them were lying on her lounger. She had to be careful, he was injured. But they were now pressed together and he kissed her again.

She felt his arm round her waist. His fingers slipped under the waistband of her shorts, stroking the skin and making her feel things that she thought had been dead for years.

Now her arms were round him, pulling him to her. She knew from the tenseness of his body exactly what he was feeling. Her lower body was clad only in the thinnest of shorts, she was wearing the skimpiest of underwear. Her body could have been naked and she knew the excitement of him.

Her breath sobbed as he took his lips from hers. His hand slid up her back, felt the clip and undid her bra and she shuddered with excitement. Then she slid down onto her back, and felt his hands easing her shirt upwards, pushing aside her bra. There was the coolness of the breeze on her now naked breasts. A moment's delicious anticipation. Then she sighed and softly cried out, her body arching as his mouth took first one, then the other rose-tipped bud. He kissed them, even tenderly bit them, she had never felt like this before.

Where would it end? At the moment she didn't care. She only knew that she wanted this, wanted him. Any consequences were not her concern. She could hear, feel the harshness of his breath and wondered, a little fearfully, what he was going to do next. Take off her shirt? If he wanted to, he could.

Then he jerked, a totally different kind of movement. For a moment, in horror, she wondered if she had rubbed against the dressing on his back, if it had been pain that had caused him to move back from her. He stood by the side of her lounger.

Then she heard it. A banging, a knocking, as on a door. And a voice that called out, 'Dad! Are you asleep or in the shower or something? Can I come in?' Johanne had woken up.

Now Amy had to open her eyes. She felt a surge of excitement as she saw his messed hair, the glitter in his eyes, his mouth so soft and so disappointed. 'My daughter,' he said. 'She didn't sleep as long as I had thought—or hoped.'

There was more knocking, a more insistent voice. 'Dad! Are you there?'

Amy swung her legs off the lounger, reached behind to fasten her bra, swept a hand through her hair. 'You'd better let her in,' she said. 'Perhaps she'd like to join us if we have another cup of tea.'

His head swooped down towards her. There was one last hard kiss. He whispered, 'This isn't finished.'

Then he shouted, 'Coming, darling.' A minute later Amy heard him say, 'We've got a visitor. We were just having a cup of tea.'

Amy smiled up at the young figure who appeared in front of her. 'Hi, Johanne. Feel better for your sleep?'

'Much better, thank you,' said Johanne, looking assessingly at the two of them.

The four of them were having breakfast the next morning when things changed. Helen, a pleasant smiling girl in charge of the kiddie reps, came to their table and asked if Elizabeth and Johanne wanted to go on a half-day coach trip. 'We're going to a place called The Ranch,' she explained. 'There's activities for all ages. We'll do a bit of horseriding—well, donkeys really. Then there are animals to pet and a big indoor funfair. Afterwards we all have fries and hamburgers.'

'I want to go!' Elizabeth promptly shouted. 'I want to ride a donkey and can I wear my new hat that Uncle Adam gave me?'

'I'd like to go as well,' Johanne said quietly. 'I've had enough of the sea for a while.'

So it was settled. 'We'll do a bit of sightseeing, shall we, Amy?' Adam said carelessly. 'There's a couple of places close by that I'd like to visit.'

'I'd like that, too,' said Amy.

Five minutes later Amy was climbing into Adam's car. She felt a little frightened, a little apprehensive. What would he say about what had nearly happened yesterday? What would he expect? For that matter, what did she want herself? She just didn't know.

But the problem didn't arise. They drove across a wide fertile plain and he chatted happily about his training, and the different skills needed by nurses and doctors. They talked about politics and discovered they more or less agreed on most things. They had different tastes in music, but didn't dislike what the other enjoyed.

After half an hour of this chat, Amy was feeling a little irritated. After an hour she was downright angry.

He was telling her what his favourite television programme was when she interrupted him and said, 'Adam! Can we stop talking like two old women on a Mothers' Union outing? We're saying nothing about...about what nearly happened yesterday. Did it mean so little to you?'

He turned to look at her. 'You know better than that,' he said. 'I just thought we'd take things easy for a while. We have most of today together, don't we?'

'Yes, I suppose we do.'

'And if it's any consolation to you, I got no sleep last night till the small hours. I lay awake, thinking about you.'

'I thought about you quite a lot,' she admitted. 'I worried and worried about how I really felt—and then I went to sleep.'

Adam smiled. 'Let's just enjoy today and we'll talk later. I thought we'd go to the Castell de Santueri, the views from there are meant to be fantastic.'

The views were fantastic. From the ruined castle they could see both Minorca and Ibiza. But by lunchtime both were exhausted. It was warmer, far warmer than it had yet been. And it was humid, sticky. There was no sun, the sky was thick with dirty grey clouds. They walked to a café, ordered iced drinks and a salad each.

'I'm glad I'm not at The Ranch,' he said. 'It'll be rough on Elizabeth and Johanne.'

Amy shook her head. 'No chance. They'll go inside where it's air-conditioned. I've talked quite a bit to Helen, she's a qualified children's nurse and the children are all properly supervised and looked after.'

Adam looked up at the sky. 'I think this weather will break.' He looked up as the waiter laid plates of salad in front of them and asked him, 'What will the weather do, do you think?'

'Tomorrow will be fresh and fine,' the waiter said. 'But I think there will be a storm and a wild night.'

'A wild night,' Adam said, and looked at her thoughtfully. Amy shivered. She wondered what he meant.

They set off back to the hotel. In spite of the car's air-conditioning their clothes were sticking to their backs. As they walked into the hotel a few giant drops of rain spattered onto the pavement.

'What I'd really like now,' Amy said, 'is a cup of your tea.' Then she realised she had invited herself to his room. Was that being forward?

Once there she felt at a bit of a loss. He was busying himself making tea, she couldn't work out whether she was happier in the room with the air-conditioning turned up full blast or outside on the balcony in the open.

She pulled fretfully at her shirt. 'Perhaps I should

have gone to my room and showered and changed,' she said.

He handed her a dressing-gown. 'Shower here if you like. Then you can sit in this, it's quite capacious. I'll finish making the tea and then we can sit outside and talk.'

She was tempted but she shook her head, 'Tea first, then perhaps I'll have a shower. And do we need to talk?'

'I think you need to more than I do,' he said. She had no answer to that.

He made the tea and she went onto the balcony, pulled up the backs of the loungers so they were two upright seats and placed them on opposite sides of the table. Then she peered round the balcony wall, checking to make sure that no one could overhear them. It seemed safe.

It was hotter, stickier than ever. The sky was a dirty grey, in the distance she could see lightning flickering over the sea.

The tea quenched her thirst, but made her feel hotter than ever.

'We have to talk,' he said again, and she sighed. She knew he was right but...

'Adam, I just don't know. You'll have to help me. I had it all worked out, how I was going to say that yesterday was just an accident, something that we had to forget. What happened then just wasn't me. I'm not promiscuous, I've only ever slept with my husband. And so I haven't slept with anyone for the past two and a half years.'

Now she had started, it seemed easier. Things came pouring out, ideas that she'd had for a long time but had mentioned to no one. 'I've wanted to sleep with people. I've had offers, and once I was very tempted. But though I hated him, though I intended to divorce him and never live with him again, Paul was still my husband. It tore me apart.'

He nodded. 'But you're a young, healthy woman. You have feelings like anyone, you've just had to hide them. Perhaps yesterday what you really wanted came out.'

'What I really wanted? I know what I really want. Adam, I like you very much, but I don't want a man in my life. I've had one, it was a disaster. I've got my life sorted out, got my job and my daughter. I'm happy now.' She thought for a minute. 'Well, I can cope now and I'm not going to jeopardise what I've got.'

He nodded again. 'I can see that, sympathise with it all. In fact, I feel the same way myself.'

He waved his hand around, indicating the hotel, the long gardens, the pools, the sea. 'The thing is, this isn't real. At home we don't dine outside every night, dance by the pool, walk by the sea. This is an unreal life and that unreality is what brought us together.'

She liked that idea. It made everything seem not quite her fault. 'So yesterday afternoon, when we—'

She just wasn't expecting it. A great streak of white lightning flashed, not in the sky but apparently right in front of her. She jerked. But somehow she caught her breath and went on 'Yesterday afternoon when we—'

And then came the thunder. It was loud, louder than ever she had heard it, as if it was there in front of her, on the balcony, in the very room. An initial crash, and then a rolling crescendo that seemed to go on and on and on.

She couldn't help herself. She screamed through sheer shock, knocked the table away and leapt for the comfort of Adam's arms. He took her, held her close to him as she gasped for breath, feeling the pounding of her heart.

Then there was a sound like cloth ripping. And the rain came pouring down, so thick it was almost hard to breathe. Instantly, both were soaked. But they were cooler. And they clung together like two spent swimmers.

She could feel the rain trickling between her breasts, making her white shirt and shorts transparent, soaking her socks and filling her shoes. She didn't mind. His arms were around her, his wet body pressed to hers.

He kissed her, one hand cupping the back of her neck, one arm around her waist. This time there was no tentative overture, no attempt to discover whether she wanted to be kissed. He knew she wanted him just as he wanted her. Their wet faces touched, and as the cool rain beat down on them they knew they had ignited a fire of their own.

She had no idea how long they stood there, taking such pleasure in each other. Now her arms were around him. She stroked his soaking back, ran her fingers around the sodden waistband of his trousers. And she felt him touching her, his hands caressing her body. It was so good—but both knew it was only a beginning.

His lips parted from hers and she looked up at his dark hair plastered to his skull, the rain dripping from his eyebrows, streaking his cheeks. And his grey eyes burned with a message that was unmistakable. 'You're wet,' he said. 'You're wet through.'

'So are you.' She felt her own hair, now lank and dripping. 'I must look a real mess.'

'You look gorgeous. And you feel...'

Lightning flashed again, not so near this time, but she still pressed against him, waiting for the soul-shaking sound of the thunder. It came. And it rolled on and on and on.

In time it finished. He relaxed his hold on her and whispered, 'Perhaps we should go inside. You need to get out of those wet clothes. I can lend you...'

Now she came to it, the decision seemed to be already made. This was happening to her, there was only now and no thought of the future, it was what she wanted. 'I need to get out of the wet clothes,' she said. 'So do you.'

No one could hear them, see them. She stepped back from him, crossed her arms, pulled shirt and bra over her head. With two hands she slid down her shorts and knickers, even managing to drag off her socks and shoes. Then she stepped back, feeling the rain beat on her naked body, feeling such pleasure in it. And then was more pleasure in seeing the shock and desire mingled in his eyes. 'Now you,' she said.

For a moment he looked even more shocked. But then he smiled, pulled off his soaking clothes with as much speed as she had done. When he was naked he reached for her again and pressed his rain-cooled body to hers.

It was like nothing she'd ever felt before. And she

knew it wasn't just the rain, the excitement of being here in the open air. It was being with Adam.

They stood, they kissed. She felt the warmth that was growing between them, knew his need for her was getting even stronger. This, she knew, was only a prelude, there was more that must come. So when he slid his arm around her waist and urged her towards the sliding glass door that opened into his room, she went willingly.

'Stand here,' he said, his voice hoarse. 'Don't move. I want to see you just like that, so stand here.'

Proudly unselfconscious, she did as he demanded. A tiny part of her mind looked on in amazement, this wasn't how the usual Amy Harrison behaved! But Amy didn't care. There was only now.

Then he led her to his bed. And it was all that she had ever dreamed of.

Afterwards, perhaps they lay in one another's arms for an hour. Then she wriggled and said, 'I'm going to fetch you some tea in bed. Then we need to carry on talking for a while.'

'I'd like the tea. I'm not so keen on the talking. Why don't you stay here a while and we'll—?'

'Adam! Tea first.'

She avoided his reaching hands and went into the kitchen. She made the tea and climbed back into bed, and for a while they sat there side by side, drinking their tea. Then he leaned over, to kiss one of her breasts and said, 'I suspect you want to talk again. But now things are different. We are lovers now, there's some kind of commitment in that. So what have you got to say to me?'

She had to get her thoughts in order. But it was much easier now, there was no overwhelming conflict between what her body told her it needed and what the cold light of reason told her.

'First,' she said, 'There's no chance of my getting pregnant. I've had a bit of a hormonal imbalance so I'm on the Pill. So no unwanted consequences.'

'There will be consequences,' he said quietly, 'there must be. One thing I have learned is that if you do something…earth-shattering like this, then there will be consequences and you have to accept them.'

Amy thought about this, it was a bit daunting. 'I think I see what you mean,' she said. 'So what consequences do you expect?'

Now it was his turn to think, but he avoided giving an answer. 'First tell me what you want,' he said.

'I'm still not sure myself. Over the past hour and a half, my life has been completely altered. There are new horizons, but they frighten me.' She mused a moment, and then went on, 'but I felt—you showed me—a happiness that I'd never known before. And that frightened me even more. But I feel I'm a woman again.'

'Oh, you certainly are,' he said, running a finger down her shoulder and onto her breast again. 'You certainly are.'

She took his hand and kissed it. 'Now you must tell me what you think, what you want,' she said.

He considered. 'In my life, the first thing must be Johanne. She had a rough time after parting from her mother, she felt she had been rejected. I'm doing the best I can for her, but I'm still not sure it's enough. I'm not in any way ashamed of what we did together,

Amy, but I don't want Johanne to know that we've slept together.'

'I agree. I have a daughter myself, she's much younger but I recognise at once what you feel.' She eased herself a little away from him. 'So we think of this as an occasion that just happened. It was so good it brought us both incredible happiness, but now we forget it.'

'No!' His voice was anguished. 'You gave me so much, I can't let you go now. We have to see each other again.'

'So, over the next few days we tiptoe around the situation, meeting furtively, grabbing a little bit of happiness when we can?'

'It'll have to be that. Can you put up with it?'

'It's not ideal. But it's so much better than not seeing you at all. We can manage somehow.'

'Whatever you think.' He put his arm round her, kissed her again. Their bodies were pressed together as they had been before, she felt the warmth of him, the rising passion. He whispered, 'So we'd better make the most of the time we have? Like now?'

She felt that now familiar sensation again, as if her body had a life of its own, knowing what it wanted and determined to have it. Slowly, she slid down the bed, easing off the towel as she did so. His head bent to her breasts again. After the first explosion of excitement, she managed to say, 'But remember what you said before. This is a holiday romance. We have eight days left and then it ends. Then we move back into the real world and it must be goodbye. I just can't, daren't start anything new now—if ever. And you're the same, aren't you?'

His hand slid from her waist, downwards. 'You can cram a lifetime into seven days,' he said.

What he said was not now important. What he was doing was important—and she sobbed with excitement.

Johanne and Elizabeth now spent so much time together they were like sisters. So it wasn't surprising how often Adam and Amy could sneak an hour or more together. Even a kiss at night, in the darkness of the garden, was worth so much. And sometimes she glanced up to see him looking at her, and as their eyes met she knew what he was thinking—or feeling. They could signal each other, say so much with the tiniest of expressions.

She had no doubts, no regrets. They were hurting no one, they lived in the present with no worries about the future. In fact, they never thought of it. But then there were only three days left.

Amy, Elizabeth and Johanne had started breakfast together. Adam had been called to Reception for some reason. When he came towards them a chill settled on Amy's heart. She could tell by his expression that it was bad news.

He sat at the table, reached for the coffee-pot. 'That was the police,' he said. 'They need a statement about that girl we pulled out of the water. She's recovered completely, by the way, but there has to be some kind of inquiry so I have to go into Palma. And since you're the first one who saw her in difficulties, Johanne, they want a statement from you, too.'

'Dad! I want to stay with Amy and Elizabeth.'

'So do I. And I suppose we could both refuse. But

giving a statement might help someone else some time in the future. It might help save a life. So I'm going to give a statement and I'd like you to do so, too.'

His voice was calm, but Amy could hear the thread of certainty underneath. Adam knew he was right. He was going to do what he thought best—no matter what.

Johanne recognised the tone of voice, too. 'OK, Dad, I'll come,' she said gloomily. 'But I can think of better ways of spending the day. The girl's alive, isn't she?'

'Elizabeth and I will look forward to seeing you both later,' Amy said. 'There'll be the evening together. Now, Adam, what are you having for breakfast?'

She felt a bit lost when he and Johanne had gone. She sat in the sun reading her book and watching Elizabeth splashing in the junior pool. She wished that Adam was somewhere near. She'd got very fond of his company.

Had she just seen a new side of him? Or had she forgotten it was there? She thought of his certainty that he was right, his decision to do what he thought best, no matter what the cost. Her dead husband had had a similar kind of certainty, and Amy had hated it. But Adam was different. Wasn't he?

Amy decided that she'd like to hear a loving voice, she needed to know she was wanted. So when Elizabeth was collected for a meeting of the Beach Babes, she went into the hotel foyer and phoned her mother. It was the first time for four days, it would be good to speak to her. But there was no answer.

Funny, she should be in at this time. Amy left a message on the answering machine and decided to try again in half an hour.

When she rang again there was no answer. She sat and thought for a minute, decided to phone the surgery. Her mother knew all the staff there, had worked with a couple of them. They might know something.

She got through to the receptionist, Rita. 'Rita, have you any idea where my mother is? I can't get through to her at home.'

Amy felt the first hint of unease when her friend didn't answer the question or ask how the holiday was going. Instead, with rather a cautious voice, she said, 'Hi, Amy. I'm putting you through to Dr Wright now.'

'Dr Wright? Rita, why Dr Wright? All I'm asking is—'

'I'm putting you through now.'

Now Amy was seriously worried. Dr Wright was an old family friend. He knew her mother very well. Why should she have to talk to—

'Amy! Good to hear from you. Enjoying your holiday?'

'Never mind that. Where's my mother? Is everything all right?'

'Everything is fine—more or less. But your mother's in hospital with pleurisy.'

Amy was a nurse as well as a daughter. 'Pleurisy? Dry or wet?'

'Wet. She had this sudden stabbing pain in her chest, called me round. I decided to be extra careful and sent her to hospital. They've drained the fluid and sent it for analysis but I'm sure everything will be fine. She'll be home in a day or two,'

'But why didn't she tell me?'

'She told us not to, she insisted that we say nothing. She said that you needed a break and that there was no need for you to rush home.'

'Well, you know I'm going to rush home, don't you?'

'Amy! There really is no need. We're all coping fine.'

'I'm coming anyway. I'll see you some time to-night.' Then she rang off.

She took a moment to consider, to remember. Pleurisy wasn't usually dangerous. The pleura was a membrane between the chest wall and the lungs. Dry pleurisy was when the membrane became inflamed; wet pleurisy—often the more dangerous kind—was when fluids collected in between the pleura and the chest wall. Dr Wright was right, it was highly unlikely that the condition was serious. It was certainly pain-ful—coughing could be agonising. But, whatever, there was no question about it. She was going home at once.

There was a travel agent rep on duty at the hotel. When Amy explained the situation to her, said it was an emergency, she nodded and phoned the airport. It took no time to organise. Amy could catch a plane in four hours, there would be a taxi waiting for her out-side the hotel in two hours.

Amy rushed back to her room and packed. She didn't want to think, she needed to act without think-ing. But after an hour her bags were ready and taken to Reception.

Elizabeth would be with the Beach Babes for another half-hour. Now Amy had to think of the situation she was abandoning—to think of Adam.

There were three days of her holiday left. She had been looking forward to spending them with Adam, but had already started wondering about how they would part. Perhaps this way was better. Sudden, rushed, no time to wonder or make foolish promises.

For a moment she wondered if she was making an excuse of her mother's illness. Pleurisy—even wet pleurisy—wasn't too dangerous. Was she using this as a means of avoiding that last painful conversation she knew she would have to have with Adam? She just didn't know.

She had taken this—well, it was a relationship, wasn't it? She had taken this relationship on as a holiday romance. They had both agreed to see each other just for a few days. Now it was over. Did she want to see more of him? Well, of course she did. But was she going to risk her future happiness by trusting another man? She just couldn't do it.

Amy took a sheet of hotel notepaper, started to write. A short, formal note to him and Johanne. An explanation, but no suggestion that they keep in touch. She would hope he had a good holiday in Canada and wish him well in his future career.

As she looked up she caught sight of herself in a mirror. Why were her eyes shining like that? Surely not tears?

CHAPTER FIVE

THAT had been then.

Seven weeks had passed in which she had tried to push Adam Ross out of her thoughts and perhaps had succeeded. Well, just a bit. It helped if she thought of it as what it was, a holiday romance, not to be taken seriously. And as she worked in and around Lissom, she came across people, places that reminded her of her ex-husband. And that made her more determined. She had thought herself desperately in love once—and look where that had got her.

And now Adam was coming to see her, alone, in her own house. Well, she could cope.

She guessed he would be punctual, it was one of the virtues he respected. And he was. Her doorbell rang at exactly eight o'clock. In spite of all her thoughts, her preparations, her rehearsals, her heart started to thud. This was going to be hard.

Somehow she opened the door and with a hostess's professional smile said, 'Adam, do come in.'

But her heart was thudding more than ever. Of course, it was colder here than in Majorca. Now he was dressed in cords, a sweater and a short leather coat. But he still looked good.

She moved back at once, she didn't want him to kiss her. He followed her into the living-room, looked round with interest. He saw the stone fireplace, the couch drawn up in front of it, the pictures of Elizabeth on the walls and the mantelshelf.

'I've brought a bottle of wine,' he said. 'You're not on call or anything?'

'No. This evening my time is my own.' She looked at the bottle he held out to her. It was one they had drunk many times at the hotel. The same as the one she had put back in the cupboard. Well, if he wanted to bring back memories... But he didn't need the wine for that. 'Take your coat off and make yourself at home,' she said. 'I have glasses ready.'

He took his coat off, but instead of sitting he walked round the room, inspecting the pictures of Elizabeth. 'Elizabeth is here?' he asked.

'Sleeping upstairs. You remember, she's a good child. Sleeps easily.'

'I remember her very well. I've missed her and so has Johanne. Could I see her?'

The question threw her. She hadn't expected this. 'No...yes...I suppose so,' she said. 'Why do you want to see her?'

'I told you, I've missed her. And, besides, I like children.'

'Well, keep very quiet, then.' She took him upstairs. They had to pass her own bedroom. She had forgotten that the door was open and he could see her double bed, her uniform still hanging on the wardrobe door. For a moment she wondered if this had been a plan to get her upstairs, then she rejected the thought. Adam wasn't like that. But she noticed he did glance in.

They stood side by side and looked at Elizabeth, who, as ever, was looking sweet. 'I remember

Johanne looking like that,' he said, 'but then she grew up.'

'They do,' said Amy.

She watched as he gently moved a wisp of hair from Elizabeth's forehead, stroked it back against her head. It looked like the act of a loving man and she didn't want to think about it. 'Let's go and have some wine,' she said abruptly. 'You can't stay long. I have a full day and I need an early start.' The sight of him apparently so pleased to see Elizabeth was upsetting.

He sat on the couch, she sat on an easy chair to one side and passed him the corkscrew. There were glasses and plates of little goodies on the coffee-table already. Silently he opened the bottle, poured the wine. They both sipped.

She felt uneasy, then she felt angry at being made to feel uneasy in her home, the home she had created with her own hands. This was her domain. He was the interloper.

'In the letter you left me you said that your mother was ill,' he said, 'and you had to get back to her.'

'She had pleurisy. I felt I had to get back and sort things out. I told you that.'

'I know. We missed you, Johanne and I, but Johanne understood when I explained to her that you were worried about your mother.'

'Johanne understood? You didn't understand?'

'I thought we meant more to each other than something that could be curtly dismissed in a letter.'

'A letter that would be read by your daughter,' she pointed out. 'The daughter you wanted not to know about us. I was sorry I had to go, I would have liked another couple of days with you. But these things happen. And I hate goodbyes. A letter was best.'

'Perhaps.' Adam was obviously not convinced.

'Adam, it was a holiday romance! We both agreed that. I didn't want anything long term, I still don't. So let's get to the question—what are you doing here?'

'It was the kind of job I was looking for when I came back from Canada,' he said. 'A pleasant town to live in, attractive countryside, apparently a very good school for Johanne. I'm renting a flat this afternoon, with the option to buy. Most important, it's a chance to do the kind of work I like best. Work I think I'm good at. I'm a doctor, Amy. This job has everything I want.'

'That's rubbish! You came here because of me!'

There was silence for a moment and then she said, 'That sounds very egocentric, very arrogant. Tell me what I said is not true and I'll apologise.'

After a while he said, 'Of course you're right. I came here largely because of you.'

'Why? D'you want more free sex?'

He flushed. 'That thought is unworthy of you, Amy,' he said. 'You know it's not true.'

'Perhaps not,' she mumbled. 'But there's another question. Why have you come when you know I don't want you here?'

'I wanted…I needed…to see more of you. It's as simple as that. I wanted to see how things still were between us. You made such an impression on me… And, Amy, I'm as unsure of things as you are.'

She drank some of the wine and tried to ignore the rush of memories that it brought about. 'It's over,

Adam. I'm at home now, with a job, a daughter, a place in the community. I don't need a man.'

'I thought that's what you did need, you seemed passionate to me. I take it there's no other man in your life? You said not.'

'No other man. And I don't want one. And if I did, Adam, you're too much like my ex-husband to be comfortable.'

She saw the glow of anger in his eyes. But his voice was still calm as he said, 'That's not a comparison I care for. How am I like him?'

'When you've made your mind up, you're always sure you are right. You have a tendency to ride over other people's feelings. If you had really thought of me, you wouldn't have come here. You know I didn't want you.'

'I came here because I just couldn't stop thinking about you. I tried, Amy, I really did. I even went out with a girl in Canada a couple of times. It just didn't work. All I could see was you.'

He looked at her with that intensity she remembered so well. 'Now, you be honest with me. Have you thought about me? Missed me?'

She couldn't lie. 'Sometimes,' she admitted. 'I missed you a lot at first. But just because you want something sometimes it doesn't mean it's good for you.'

'Perhaps not.' He took another sip of wine, rolled the glass between his hands. 'I'm going to admit to what you've accused me of,' he said. 'When I see something I want, I go for it, and sometimes I don't bother too much about the consequences. And, Amy, I think I want you. We both need time to decide. But

I thought that with you I had the chance of happiness I'd never seen before.'

'You said your ex-wife had made you suspicious of any relationships!'

'I did. I meant it, perhaps I still do mean it. Sometimes I can't believe what I'm doing now. We've known each other for such a short time, we'd be mad to start anything.'

'In this case it takes two to start something,' she pointed out.

'True. But we're going to work together for six months. We'll get to know each other better and perhaps we'll both come to see that there's something in it for us both.'

'It won't happen! I don't want it to happen! Adam, why did you have to come here? You're upsetting me.'

She had intended to remain calm, to be mistress of the situation. But what he was saying was making that almost impossible. She knew her plea had affected him. There was the anguish in his face. But then it was replaced by determination.

'The last thing I want to do is to cause you pain. I want you to be happy. I want you to find out if you could be happy with me.'

She finished her drink, stood and looked at him. He rose, too. 'I think you'd better go now,' she said. 'Please, don't ever come here again unless I ask you to. Don't phone me here, we can talk at work. This is my home, my refuge. I need somewhere that's safe.'

'You're safe with me!' Then his face fell and he said, 'But I guess I'd better go.'

He picked up his coat, made for the door. He reached for the doorhandle, and before she knew what he was doing he stooped and kissed her. She wasn't expecting it, wasn't prepared. So, without thought, she kissed him back. For a moment they were back in Majorca, hiding in the shadows in the garden, snatching a moment of stolen pleasure. But then she pushed him away.

They were close. She could see the turmoil in his eyes and wondered what he could see in her eyes.

'You know, you wanted to kiss me then,' he said gently, 'just as much as I wanted to kiss you.'

'Yes, I know. It brought back memories. Paul used to do that, kiss me until my legs felt weak. Then I married him and he bullied me. He harassed me, even hit me once, made my life a complete misery. So it made the memory of that kiss a bit sour.'

She saw the shock on his face. She opened the door, he passed through it and she closed it before he could even say good-night. She waited behind the door. After a moment she heard the crunch of footsteps moving away. He had gone.

She didn't want to think, she needed to work. So she went back to the living-room, cleared away. But that didn't take long so she sat down and asked herself why her heart was still beating so rapidly.

That kiss. It had meant so much to her. She shied away from making comparisons, it seemed unfair to both concerned. But secretly she had to admit to herself that that lovemaking with Adam had brought her more fulfilment than she had ever felt with Paul. It wasn't just that Adam was more considerate, it was something to do with her own feelings. She realised that she had been just a child with Paul. With Adam she was a woman.

Just once, in a moment of sheer self-indulgence, she remembered what it was like to be in his arms. She thought about what it would be like to share a life with him, see his face smiling at her from the pillow every morning. Dinner together every night, perhaps even a brother or sister for Johanne and Elizabeth... Elizabeth! That brought her up short. She had Elizabeth to think of, apart from herself. But, then, he and Elizabeth had got on so well together.

Adam didn't want to drive home at once. He knew that Johanne would be quite happy on her own for the next hour or so as she'd got a video she particularly wanted to watch. He had allowed himself plenty of time, now he had to acknowledge that there was a part of him that had been wondering—hoping—that he might have stayed longer with Amy. That their meeting might have gone a little better.

There was a river running through the centre of Lissom. On each bank was a little park, with flower-beds and benches. He left his car and walked along the river. Then, by a weir, he sat and for a moment his head was filled with nothing but the peaceful rattle of the water. He looked up. It was a clear night, the first stars were coming out. He liked this town. Or did he just like the town because Amy was here?

What exactly did he want of Amy? The meeting hadn't gone all that well—but not too badly either. When he had kissed her he had felt her reaction, had known that she had needed—wanted—the kiss. Almost as much as he had. Well, that was a start.

He wondered if she knew just how honest he had been with her. Certainly he had come here to be a doctor—and he knew that he was going to enjoy his professional life. It was a good, dedicated practice and he could think of nothing better than working with the team. But his basic reason for coming had been to find Amy, to see her again. But, as he had told her, he was still unsure as to what he wanted.

Her question about him just wanting free sex had been unfair, he wanted far more than that. But he had to admit that she had showed him a world, an experience that in his own marriage he had never known existed.

His marriage! He had thought he had been in love with his wife. Just how wrong had he been? Could a relationship with Amy turn out to be just as disastrous? Possibly. He didn't know.

He sighed. How many times had he been over this ground in the past few weeks? He thought he could be happy with Amy. Six months should be long enough to find out. That was, if she was still interested.

Next day was a normal working day. Whatever emotional turmoil Amy might be going through, life had to go on. So it was breakfast with Elizabeth, uniform on and drive round to her mother's.

Elizabeth was the first child there, and went instantly to play by herself in a corner. Amy's mother was just finishing her breakfast. Amy had kept an eye on her since her illness, but she seemed to have recovered. Now she was looking well. There was a brightness in her eyes.

Obviously she was enjoying her work, she loved children. She would have liked a larger family, but after having Amy she had developed an infection that had made having more babies a very risky business.

Amy hadn't told her mother about her affair. In fact, apart from Adam, no one knew. And since her mother had been ill when Amy had returned from her holiday, she hadn't questioned her daughter too much about how she had enjoyed herself. Amy preferred it that way.

'You're looking well,' she said to her mother, 'not only completely recovered but better than you were before.'

'Everyone should have a stay in hospital. It makes you grateful for what you've got. You appreciate it more.'

'It's a point of view,' Amy agreed. 'But I think I'd rather stay out of a hospital bed.'

Then it was off for her day's work. Every day was similar, every day was different. Her first visit was to an elderly lady who had been rushed into hospital with appendicitis. Now that she'd been discharged, Amy was changing her dressings, making sure she didn't relapse in any way.

There was another old lady to help get washed, a couple of injections to give. Then a drive out into the countryside to Laneside Farm. This was a case—one of many—where Amy was a social worker as much as a nurse.

Laneside Farm was large, the white-painted farmhouse standing on the lane that gave it its name, a well-tended garden in front. No walking through the farmyard to get to the front door here. To one side was a cottage, with a Land Rover outside. Amy frowned. Peter Brooks drove everywhere in that vehicle. What was it doing here in the middle of the day?

The farm was owned by Nathan Brooks. His son Peter worked for him, lived in the cottage Amy was visiting. Her patient was Peter's wife, Nancy. Nancy was a bright young woman. A few days before she had been working in one of the barns and had slipped and gashed her side really badly. An ambulance had taken her to hospital, she had been given blood, her side sutured. When she had returned home the doctor—and Amy in her turn—had impressed on her the absolute importance of not in any way pulling the stitches. Nancy had to take life very easy for a week or two. And, of course, she was now bored.

Amy had stayed perhaps longer than she should have. Nancy had needed some kind of break—and her husband was no great conversationalist. The two women had talked about the people they knew—and Nancy had talked about when she should start a family. She was keener than Peter.

Amy banged on the door, walked straight in as she had been told to do. Nancy was sitting in the living-room, stretched out on the couch, a blanket over her legs. Good, she was obeying instructions. She smiled as Any entered. 'I'm so glad you've come. I need cheering up,' she said. 'I'm going mad, just sitting here.'

'Just a few more days and then you can think about starting work again,' Amy told her. 'Light work only, mind. Now, pull your sweater up and let's have a look.'

Nancy's wound was progressing nicely. Amy cleaned it, put on a new dressing. 'I see the Land Rover's outside,' she said. 'What's Peter doing for transport?'

'Peter's off work, he's in bed. He's been really off colour. He had a few drinks at the rugby club a couple of nights ago and has been feeling rotten ever since. It must be a really bad cold, or perhaps it's flu. Anyway, whenever I ask, he shouts at me.'

'Want me to go and have a look at him?' Amy asked.

'Would you? In fact, I have been quite worried about him. I've never seen him as bad as this before.'

'I'll just say hello.' Amy didn't particularly want to say hello to Peter. She'd known him for years but she didn't much like him. Once he'd even made a pass at her. Not that that was something special. Peter made passes at anything in a skirt.

But when she went into the bedroom, she found him in a bad way. For once he didn't object to her questioning him, even examining him. He was generally low. He had a rash and a high temperature. He complained of pains in his joints but Amy could find no swelling. She felt uneasy. She'd seen many cases of flu. This wasn't one of them. 'I'd like to get the doctor out to look at you,' she said. For once, the big tough farmer didn't object.

Amy slipped outside and phoned the surgery. She was in luck. Rita said that Dr Wright was between patients and Amy could speak to him at once. 'If you're calling, it must be an emergency,' the senior partner said. 'What's the problem?'

Carefully, Amy went over the symptoms. She

didn't say what she thought was wrong, it was the doctor's job to diagnose. But he asked her anyway. 'What do you think is wrong?'

'I wondered—hepatitis?'

'Hmm,' said Dr Wright. 'That could open a can of worms. Tell you what, I'll ask our new doctor to come out. He's still being inducted, but it will be good for him to see the kind of work we do. Can you make a visit with him this afternoon?'

She told herself that having to make calls with Adam was the kind of thing that was going to happen so she had to get used to it. 'Of course I can,' she said.

'Good. And you may as well take him on the rest of your round. Get him to know the place and a few of our regular patients. That OK?'

'No trouble at all.'

A bit of her was glad. This had to be faced up to. She'd get it over quickly, the sooner the better.

There was an auction of animals in the cattle market that afternoon and the streets of Lissom were crammed with lorries and trailers carrying cargoes of sheep and cattle. The presence of Adam beside her in her four-wheel-drive didn't worry her at first. Like her, he remained silent. But soon they were out of town, threading their way through the maze of white-walled fields that she knew so well. And she thought she ought to make a statement.

'It's a friendly surgery,' she said. 'I'm sure you've seen we all get on well.'

'Of course,' he said.

'I love my work here. I'm very happy in it and I

want to stay that way. I suspect you'll be doing a lot of house calls often with me. I think that if we are polite to each other, we can work around this situation. We can forget what happened before. We'll be colleagues.'

'Of course we will. But, Amy, things happened between us. And you know they were important to us both. We might not speak of them, but no way can I forget them. Neither, I suspect, can you.'

'Too bad. We'll have to do the best we can, won't we? Now, I don't want to say any more about it.'

She swerved around a bunch of cyclists. 'Shouldn't be two abreast in this narrow lane,' she muttered. 'Now, the case we're going to see. It could be nothing or it could be a bad case of flu, but I doubt it. I've never seen a fit young man look so low. He's a big rugby player, quite a good amateur. In fact, he went with his team on a tour of the Far East some months ago, and I gather they did quite well.'

'D'you know exactly where they went?' His voice was suddenly alert.

'No. But I gather they had a good time.'

'A good time in the Far East. Any chance he might have been taking drugs?'

She laughed. 'No chance. The only drug he's interested in is alcohol.'

'You're thinking what I am,' he said. 'I hope you're wrong, though.'

'Me, too. I like his wife, she's lovely. She deserves—'

'Don't jump the gun,' he said.

Amy helped him with his examination. He did

practically the same as she had done, and then said
formally, 'I'd like to see the patient alone now, Amy.'

'Of course.'

He joined her perhaps ten minutes later, when she
was sitting chatting to Nancy. 'Mrs Brooks, I've ordered an ambulance and I've phoned the hospital telling them to expect your husband. We need to have
tests done. I suspect that your husband is suffering
from some kind of blood or kidney infection.'

Nancy looked confused. 'An infection? What kind
of an infection? How did he get it?'

'We just don't know. We won't know very much
until we get the results from the hospital lab. Then
I'll come back and tell you. It could be serious but I
doubt it will be fatal.'

'Just what kind of disease could he pick up
abroad?' asked Nancy.

But then they heard the sound of an engine outside,
and Amy saw the white side of an ambulance. Adam
went to watch Peter being carried out on a stretcher,
and shortly afterwards they left the farm. 'Where
now?' Adam asked.

'Now we have to go to see Sadie. A totally different kind of case. Sadie is eighty-nine and lives alone.
She has a good care worker but she cooks all her own
meals. I help her wash and see that everything is fine
with her. You'll like Sadie and she'll like you. She
likes all doctors—except female ones.'

Adam smiled.

They drove on in silence for a while and then she
said, abruptly, 'You thought hepatitis B?'

'Yes, I did. Of course we both may be wrong, I
hope so. How come you spotted it so quickly?'

'I came across a few cases when I worked in A and E. Drug addicts mostly.'

He mused, 'That's the commonest way of catching it. Infected blood, dirty needles. It can be transmitted by a human bite if the skin is broken.'

'Don't mess me about, Adam,' she said bitterly. 'We both know what the most likely cause is. Sexual contact. Probably in the Far East, where it's almost pandemic.'

'I asked him. It is a possibility. Said he was drunk at the time.'

'So what about poor Nancy? She wants a baby soon. Instead, tomorrow I give her an injection to protect her from her husband. I've done my public health courses. If he has hepatitis B, there's a one in ten chance that he'll be a carrier. There's a one in ten chance the condition could become chronic, which would lead to cirrhosis of the liver. And Nancy has to live with that. Isn't it great to be a man? Visit some prostitute, bring back the results to the family.'

'You're jumping the gun, Amy. We don't know what he's got yet.'

'True. But it's what you think.'

'And not all men are the same, Amy. It's wrong to generalise.'

Amy took a deep breath to calm herself and then said, 'Of course not. I agree with you, we must stay detached. We must never make moral judgements, it's not our job. But you learn things, find you have ideas that are impossible to get rid of. And it's just too bad.'

'We're not talking about Peter here, are we?' he asked after a while.

'No. We're talking about me.'

He was silent for a while and then said, 'Life is a learning process. People should progress. I can't help thinking that it's...sad if you take up a position early in life and then never question it. Things, people can change.'

'Are we still talking about me?' she asked sharply. 'I'm not sure I want your opinions on how I should change.'

He didn't get angry, either with her remark or her tone. 'We're only partly talking about you. We're talking about people in general, and specifically about me as much as you. When we met, Amy, we were both set in our opinions. I'm starting to change and I suspect you are, too. Love, kindness, thinking of someone other than yourself, generosity of spirit, they're all possible.'

'Well, thank you. I'll ask you again, Adam, just what do you want of me?'

'I want you to accept that I'm me, not someone else. And that now I like you a lot. And that we should just see how things go.'

'It's a lot to ask,' she said.

Amy didn't see much of Adam for a while. He was following his induction programme, to show him how the surgery liked to conduct its business. But they had one case they worked on together, that of Peter Brooks. The results came through. Peter did have hepatitis B.

They went together to talk to Nancy, who burst into tears. Amy was angry. Adam, wisely, said very little.

A week or so later he met her in the surgery car park. As he approached her she could see that he was apprehensive, as if not sure of how she would greet him. Well, he should know better, they were professionals.

'I'd like a quick word,' he said, 'about something personal.' Then obviously responding to her forbidding expression, he added with a sardonic grin, 'No, it's not that.'

She felt rather ashamed, they ought to be able to be friends. 'What is it, Adam?'

'Perhaps you don't fancy this—I'm a bit in doubt myself. You know I've taken a flat for six months? It's quite pleasant but it's not where I ultimately want to live. Well, Johanne's now in school, having a bit of difficulty settling. And she'd love it if you and Elizabeth would come round for an early tea some time. Honestly, Amy, though I'd love it, too, this is for her not for me.'

Amy thought for a moment and then said, 'All right, we'll come. For Johanne, not for you.'

'That'll be great. This moving about has been a shock for Johanne. She's quiet and I think she's finding school hard.'

'It's got a good reputation,' said Amy. 'I went there.'

When she set off to visit with Elizabeth, Amy had to admit she was curious. She knew the area, it was quite well-to-do. Adam had leased a flat in a new block, built in the garden of a now demolished old house.

They arrived with the necessary large box to keep Elizabeth occupied. Dolls and teddies and a little plastic teaset. They were about to ring the doorbell when the door opened and there was Johanne. 'I've been looking out for you,' she said, and gave Amy a quick kiss. 'Hello, Elizabeth, remember me? I'm Johanne.'

'Remember you,' said Elizabeth, 'We had to leave and you weren't there. But I've brought my teddies and a tea-set.'

A voice said, 'Please, come inside.' There was Adam, smiling first at Elizabeth. 'Hello, Elizabeth.'

'Uncle Adam,' Elizabeth shouted, opening her arms for a hug. 'I want to ride on the big fish again.'

Once inside the flat Johanne and Elizabeth settled down to play as if it had been yesterday that they had parted, not weeks before. Soon they were sitting on the floor together, the dolls and teddies sitting round them in a circle and the tea-set laid out. 'Would Mr Teddy like a cup of tea?' asked Johanne.

'Certainly, please,' Elizabeth said proudly.

Since Johanne was occupied it was Adam who fetched the tea things, he had them all prepared. And when they sat round the table Elizabeth sat on one of his knees and placed a teddy on the other. 'Teddy and me want to sit and have our tea with you,' she said.

'Then I'll get Teddy some bread and butter.' Adam carefully cut up a slice of bread and then placed it on the tiny plastic plate that Elizabeth had brought to the table.

Elizabeth giggled and reached for the bread herself. 'Teddy doesn't really eat things,' she told Adam confidentially.

Amy couldn't quite make out her own feelings as she watched Elizabeth and Adam together. Adam so obviously was enjoying playing with Elizabeth. And she felt that it wasn't put on for her benefit. Adam would be a fine…a fine father, his pleasure in Elizabeth's company was obvious.

Then Amy managed to put a name to the odd emotion she was feeling, the faint feeling of irritation. It was jealousy! Adam should be paying attention to her, not to her daughter! But it still was rather nice to see the two of them together.

For most of the time while they were eating she talked to Johanne about school. There were teachers there she remembered, customs that Johanne found a bit strange but which to Amy were normal. Johanne seemed to be finding her feet there.

'Made any new friends at school yet?' Amy asked.

'One or two,' Johanne said evasively. 'Nobody really special.'

After tea Johanne said she would wash up, and that Elizabeth could help her. Since Elizabeth loved nothing more than to be wrapped in a large pinafore and to stand on a stool and stir a large bowl of sudsy water, this offer was accepted. Amy and Adam retired to the far end of the living-room. They sat in easy chairs facing each other.

'That was cunning,' Amy said happily. 'You just brought us here to show how we could all work together as a happy family.'

'Nothing could have been further from my mind,' he said, lying quite shamelessly. 'But since we're getting on well, I thought you'd like to look at these. They're from our holiday.' He put a packet of photographs on the coffee-table between them.

'I love photographs,' said Amy.

She hadn't realised what an effect the photographs would have on her. There were simple shots of them on the beach, by the pool, sitting at dinner. Johanne had insisted on taking a lot of them, so there were more than a few of Amy sitting with Adam.

For a moment or two, as she looked through the pictures, Amy was transported back to a happier, simpler time. She had enjoyed herself so much there, it made the greyness of her present life seem even more unsupportable.

'That's a good shot,' Adam said. 'Johanne took it.' His voice seemed casual, but Amy could detect a thread of meaning in it. The photograph was of Adam and herself, sitting at a table by the pool. Adam was holding a dozing Elizabeth on his lap, her head cradled on his chest.

Amy felt her heart starting to beat a little faster. In the photograph she and Adam were looking at each other, smiling. But in the look, in that smile, there was so much meaning. Surely even the young Johanne could detect what they were feeling for each other?

'It is a good shot,' Amy said, her voice rather high. 'But then, that was a good camera you had, wasn't it?'

'People make pictures, not cameras. Can you remember how you were feeling when that was taken?'

She had to be honest. 'Yes. I was feeling…contented and happy. I could have stayed in that mood for ever.'

'Me, too. D'you think we could be that way again?'

Amy shook her head in distress. 'I'd like to say yes but…that was on holiday. A time away from real life. Now we're back in real time and I—'

'Dishes is all done,' Elizabeth shouted from a couple of feet away, and Amy jumped. How had her daughter crept up on her? 'Uncle Adam, Johanne says can we open the box, please? That box there.'

'You certainly can. Get Johanne to help you lift it out.'

For a while there was much rustling of paper and consideration of diagrams. But eventually everything was clear and assembled. On the edge of a narrow table was balanced a tiny theatre, perhaps eighteen inches high. There were curtains of red velvet, a back-cloth of a fairy castle. And from behind the theatre came the whispering of voices.

Finally, all was ready. Elizabeth's hidden voice announced, 'this is the story of Princess Elizabetha and the giant and the witch and the prince.'

The princess appeared on stage—a tiny figure stuck on the end of Elizabeth's finger, with long golden pigtails. 'I am the princess and I am very unhappy,' a voice said in a princess-like fashion.

Another finger appeared, all in black and with a pointed black hat. 'And I am the wicked witch of Lissom,' it intoned.

'There aren't any witches in Lissom,' Elizabeth said in her normal voice. 'Are there, Johanne?'

'Well, no. But we can pretend, can't we?'

'It's all right if we pretend.'

It was a good play, and Adam and Amy applauded at the end. 'Did you buy that for Johanne?' Amy whispered.

'No. I bought it for Elizabeth. I thought she might like to come here and play with it.'

'Hmm. That means you expect us to come back.'

'That'll be your choice. But you know there'll always be a welcome for you.'

'I think that's what I'm afraid of,' said Amy.

Next day Amy went to pick up Elizabeth later than usual. Adam had given her copies of all the photographs he had taken of their holiday. Amy had taken out the one of her sitting with Adam and slipped it into one of her bedroom drawers. But now she showed the rest to her mother.

'That holiday did you good,' her mother said. 'I knew it would. Who's the man?'

Amy knew she'd have to say something eventually. 'His name's Adam Ross and his daughter is Johanne. Adam has just…joined the practice as a locum for six months.'

'Ah,' said her mother.

Amy searched for something to say to avoid further questions. She noticed her mother was ironing a new dress. 'Where are you going tonight? Out with the Third Age club again?'

Her mother looked a bit flushed. She said, almost defiantly, 'Not really—in fact not at all. I'm going to the opera house at Buxton, having dinner first. I'm going with a man I met at the Third Age club.'

Amy remembered the new hairstyle, the definite sparkle in her mother's eyes. 'Ma! You've got a date!'

Amy's father had died fifteen years ago after a tragically short illness, perhaps the tragedy had pulled the two women together. Now Amy looked at her mother with new eyes, seeing her as a woman, not just her mother and Elizabeth's grandmother.

Sylvia Harrison was attractive. She was slim, through attendance at the gym and weekend walking. Her dark hair was well styled, she always dressed well.

'We're just going out together,' said her mother. 'You have to move on.'

'He's a lucky man, taking you out. Is it…are you…serious?'

Her mother thought. 'I'm interested,' she said. 'I like him a lot. And he's interested, too.'

'So who is he and when do I get to meet him?'

'His name's Noel Carson, he's a solicitor who's just moved into the area. That big firm on the main road. Now, I'm not saying anything more at all. Off you go, I'll have to get ready.'

'I'll want to know all about it tomorrow,' Amy threatened.

Her mother smiled sweetly. 'I'll tell you all about it. When you tell me all about you and this Dr Adam Ross.'

Amy was shocked at this. Would she never stop being transparent to her mother?

Next evening Amy was back at her old school, Lissom Allgates. Dr Wright knew the headmistress, and had arranged for Amy to give a series of talks on first aid after the end of the official school day. Amy enjoyed the work. The children were boisterous at times, but seemed interested in what she had to say.

It was getting dark as Amy drove away from the school as she had stopped behind to have a cup of tea with the headmistress. But there were still a few pupils walking home. She was approaching a park entrance, saw a couple come out of the park and stand in the shadow of a tree, kissing. Kissing passionately. They were in uniform, from Lissom Allgates school. And as Amy drove past them, she saw that the girl was Johanne.

Amy pulled up after a few yards, waited as Johanne walked past her. She had her arm round the boy, his was round her. The two looked happy, contented with each other. Amy felt a pang—of what? She remembered being a schoolgirl herself, she had had a boyfriend, Patrick Sheldon. Just being with him had made her happy, when they'd been apart she'd dreamed about him for hours. Now sometimes she saw Peter. He had taken over his father's outdoor equipment shop, he was going bald and had a wife and two children. They still smiled at each other when they met.

Reluctantly, and with a smile to herself, Amy had to acknowledge her feelings. She felt envious. It had been so nice to be young, in love and free from troubles—though, as she remembered, they had thought they had troubles.

But that had been then. She drove on a little, stopped again just ahead of the couple, and as they came up to her she wound down her window and said, 'Hello, Johanne.'

She tried to be friendly, but she suspected that her voice was rather cool.

Johanne was shocked. 'Amy! What are you doing here?'

'I've been giving a talk at the school.' She peered at the boy, a tall blond lad. 'You were in my class, weren't you?'

The boy was nervous. 'Yes, Miss Harrison. I'm Jack Collis. I enjoyed your talk.'

'So you'll be sixteen or seventeen. A bit old for Johanne?'

Defiantly, Johanne said, 'He's seventeen. So what? Jack and I have just met and we like each other a lot.'

Amy decided to get out of the car. They couldn't have any kind of a conversation through a window, and she still wasn't sure what she wanted to say. Perhaps it just wasn't her business. But to think that was just avoiding things.

She walked round the car, offered her hand. 'Nice to meet you Jack,' she said.

He shook her hand. 'You, too, Miss Harrison,' he said. Obviously he, too, didn't know what to make of the situation. After a moment he said, 'I really do like Johanne a lot, you know.'

Amy sighed. This had to be said. 'How much older than her are you?' she asked.

'Two years seven months and four days,' Johanne said quickly, 'and it doesn't matter one little bit. Amy, I thought you were my friend. Can't you accept that I know what I'm doing? Can't you let me make up my own mind about something without interfering?'

'I'm not interfering, Johanne, and I hope I'm still your friend. I'm also a friend of your father.'

There was silence for a moment and then, in a dead voice, Johanne said, 'So you're going to tell him. He'll stop me seeing Jack just because you saw us—'

'Kissing,' said Amy. 'And kissing quite passionately. No, I'm not going to tell him I've seen you together. But I think you should.'

'You know what'll happen if I do!'

Amy sighed again and turned to Jack. 'You know she's a child still and the law thinks that you're a responsible adult? You know what I'm talking about?'

She was rather pleased with the touch of anger in Jack's voice. 'Yes, I do know what you're talking about. I care about Johanne and I am responsible.'

'I hope so,' said Amy. Then she got in the car and drove off.

She wasn't happy. She knew how important trust was to Adam, knew that he would expect her to tell him about Johanne. She felt that she was betraying him by promising Johanne not to tell him. But she would be betraying Johanne if she did tell.

Amy sighed. She had enough trouble with her own love life. Why should she have to worry about someone else's?

CHAPTER SIX

IT WAS an unusual telephone call, from Nancy Brooks. Amy had been to see her once since she'd been to give Nancy her vaccination after Peter's disease had been diagnosed. Nancy had been angry and bitter. She didn't sleep at night, she wept most of the day. And there was nothing Amy could say to calm her. In the end she had cautiously offered to ask if Nancy could be prescribed something for depression, or just sleeping pills. Nancy had turned down the offer.

Now Nancy was calmer. 'Got a favour to ask you, Amy,' she said. 'Not really part of your job, but it might help things along.'

'Whatever I can do, Nancy, I will.'

Now Nancy seemed a little awkward. 'This is difficult. It's not only you that's involved, it's that Dr Ross as well.'

'I'm sure Dr Ross will be only too pleased to help,' Amy said, being quite certain that this was true.

Nancy spoke in a rush. 'Well, it's Peter. He's recovering now and we are at least talking. He's been really ill and I think it might have taught him something.'

'People often seem a bit different when they're recovering,' Amy said cautiously.

'Yes, I thought that. But…anyway, Peter says he's learned his lesson. He knows he's been thoughtless and stupid and he's going to try to be better. But he wants to see you and Dr Ross in hospital. He thinks talking to you both might…might help him. Amy, it's worth a try. Can you manage to go and see him? It'd mean such a lot to me.'

'But what does he want us to do? He's in hospital now, we can't interfere.'

'I don't know! But it seems to be important to him.'

'I'll see what I can do,' said Amy.

She caught Adam later that day and told him about the phone call. 'It'll mean an evening visit,' she said. 'It's not really our job and I don't know what he wants but…'

Adam shrugged. 'The little I saw of Nancy, I liked. I must say, patient or not, I didn't have much time for Peter. But if Nancy thinks it might help—well, it's only a couple of hours, isn't it? Tonight OK?'

'Sure. I'll leave Elizabeth with my mother. It'd be silly to take two cars, d'you want me to pick you up?'

'Let me drive,' he said.

Peter Brooks was in the infectious diseases ward in a Sheffield hospital. Amy had phoned ahead, said that they were coming. Peter was in a side-ward on his own.

'It's very good of you to come,' he said.

'Nancy asked us to,' said Amy. 'She said that you wanted to see us both. We're still not sure why, you know that the hospital is looking after you now.'

Peter looked uncomfortable. Amy had always known him as a big, muscular man, certain of his strength and certain that he was right. There had been no place for self-doubt in his mind. But now things were different. His face was thinner. Peter was in an environment he couldn't dominate and he didn't like it.

'I've had time to think while I've been in here,' he said. 'The nurses and doctors have been great. It looks like I'm going to be all right, eventually I should be as fit as before. But it didn't have to happen that way. One of the doctors spent half an hour with me telling me just what might have happened, what I could be suffering.' He swallowed. 'And what I could have done to Nancy,'

'Nancy will be all right,' Adam said. 'We've checked her over, she'll be fine. That's one thing you don't have to worry about.'

'But I could have…that is, she might have…she could have been infected.'

'Yes,' said Adam flatly.

'Right. Well, you're my doctor and Amy here is the district nurse who first decided I was really ill. I feel I owe you both something. What I want to say is…it won't happen again. I've been a selfish, drunken lout, but I'm going to change. Being ill has terrified me. Nancy has said she'll stand by me. I don't deserve that but I'll accept it. I just want you two to know. Things will be different. And if I start to slip you can remind me of this conversation. But I won't slip.'

'It's easy to say that now,' Adam said. 'How will you feel when you're well again?'

Peter shook his head. 'It isn't easy now. Usually I just don't admit I'm wrong. It's something I'll have to get used to.'

There was silence for a moment, then Amy took

his hand and said, 'You've got a lot to come home to, haven't you? Nancy's one in ten thousand. You're lucky.'

'I know I'm lucky.' Peter tried to smile. 'And when I'm completely better—then it'll be baby time. It's what she wants and I guess it's what I need.'

He lay back against the pillow, obviously fatigued by what he had said.

'I think we'd better go now,' said Adam. 'We don't want to overtire you.' He held out a hand for Peter to shake. Rather surprised, Peter took it. Adam went on, 'I think you can do it, Peter. What you've just said to us now took some saying, I appreciate that. But people can change for the better, I know. Good luck.'

He took Amy's arm and led her towards the door. Just before they left Amy turned. Peter's head was on the pillow again. But there was a smile on his face. He looked content.

Amy had to direct Adam out of Sheffield, but soon they were high on the moors, the city only a yellow glow on the horizon behind them. The driving was easy here, they could talk.

'You've known him longer,' said Adam. 'D'you think he'll stick to what he said?'

Amy sighed. 'Who can tell? Certainly he's not himself now. Perhaps it's only finding himself weak and defenceless that has made him like this. When he's fully recovered, who can tell what he'll feel?'

'I think he meant it,' said Adam. 'What's more, I think he'll stick to it. He's done something pretty terrible to Nancy—and to himself. I think he hates himself now and the only way he'll be able to look into a mirror again is if he changes.'

'You really believe that, don't you? That it's possible to change?'

His voice was determined, forceful. 'You have to believe that people can change. Otherwise there's no hope of redemption.'

'And once again we're not talking about Nancy and Peter. We're talking of you and me.'

'That's right. We're both carrying some pretty heavy baggage. A great load of doubt and suspicion. But I think we're moving towards being different people. Perhaps people who can be happy together. Don't you feel that, Amy?'

'It's possible,' she said.

Three days later Dr Wright called a small unofficial meeting at lunchtime. There was the practice manager, the other practice partner and a couple of the nurses. And there was Adam. Amy hadn't seen him for a day or two. She missed him, but she'd managed. Now they smiled at each other in a friendly manner.

'Many of our biggest problems aren't really medical,' John Wright said. 'This is one of them. You all know that I'm friendly with the headmistress of Lissom Allgates school and that Amy works there sometimes? Well, the headmistress phoned me. She wants Amy to give practical talks on contraception, to under sixteens as well as over sixteens. We all know what the practice policy is, that we can offer sexual advice to someone under sixteen once we have satisfied ourselves that it is in the child's best interests to have that advice. And we take considerable care to establish the child's best interests. But this is offering detailed advice to a whole group. What do you all think?'

The practice manager said, 'I'm in favour of anything that might keep the teenage pregnancy rate down. Go for it.'

The other practice partner said, 'I go with the practice policy. We offer advice when it's in the best interests of our patients. We do not go round offering it without being asked.'

Now it was Adam's turn. So far Amy had looked anywhere but at him directly, now she stared at him. She didn't like what she saw. He had the expression she recognised —that he thought he was right and that no one would deflect him.

He said, 'I'm against these talks. I have a teenage daughter at that school, and I shall expect to be asked if I want her to receive detailed practical contraceptive advice. And I shall say no. I'm very happy for her to have sex education and for contraception to be dealt with in a general way. But if you show specific contraceptives you are bound to make students think that it is OK to use them.'

He turned to her. 'What do you think, Amy?'

It was an awful moment. She realised that he expected her to agree with him. She muttered, 'That is a point of view. There is no good answer. But I suspect most young teenagers have the sense not to experiment. And if just one girl is prevented from getting pregnant, that is something good.'

His voice was silky. 'And what if, because of your expert advice, a child decides she has nothing to worry about? It was taught in school so it must be all right?'

She had to fight back. 'If—and I'm not very keen—I give these talks, I shall emphasise that it is dangerous to experiment, and that sex should only take place in the context of a loving relationship.'

'Exactly! These children have no sense. They think they're in love when all that is happening is that their adolescent glands are working overtime. I thought you'd know better, Amy.'

She looked at him and snarled, 'I know only too well the effects of glands working overtime.'

'It appears that we can't agree,' Dr Wright said smoothly. 'We've had a frank exchange of views, now I shall think about it myself and canvass other points of view. Nothing will be decided for a while. Now I guess it's back to work.'

As they walked out, Adam moved to Amy's side. He said, 'You know, I am surprised at you. You know Johanne, would you give her this talk?'

She stood a moment, trying to order her whirling thoughts. Then she said, 'This tends to be an area for nurses and midwives rather than doctors. And do you know what? The young girls most likely to get pregnant are usually the uninformed children of repressive parents. Parents who don't trust them. Think of that, Dr Ross.'

Then she hurried to get away from him. She hated the expression of horror on his face.

They had to work together a couple of days later. Bert and Doris Machin had lived together in their house for fifty-five years. Bert had been born there. It was

an old house and now it just wasn't suitable for them.
Doris had incipient Alzheimer's disease, Bert had ar-
thritis. They would have to move.

Both of them accepted this, were even looking forward to it. Amy had worked hard with both of them,
had involved her friend in Social Services. But now
there were forms to be filled in, decisions to be made,
Social Services informed officially.

Adam came with Amy. She had been visiting the
couple for three years now, and they were friends.
But the report they were asked for would have to be
signed by a doctor. So Adam came, had a cup of tea,
chatted amiably and looked around the house. Bert
and Doris liked him. They agreed that what had been
decided was best. And then Adam and Amy left.

He said nothing as they drove back towards
Lissom. She couldn't help comparing his present silence with the kindness and thought he had showed
to the couple they had just left behind. And she decided she was not going to put up with it. This was
an area she knew well, so she turned off the main
road in the valley and drove upwards along a narrow
winding lane that led to the top of the fell.

'This isn't the quickest way back,' he said after a
minute.

'No, it's not. But for the moment it's the way I
want.'

They reached the top of the fell, she turned off the
road onto a grassy area, wrenched on the handbrake
and said to him, 'You need to get out now.'

So he got out. She walked for twenty yards, hoping
he would follow her. And then she stopped, and he
came to stand by her side. They were standing on the

edge of the valley, and in front of them was a vista of fields, woods and crags. There were villages, a corner of Lissom itself.

She pointed. 'There was a Bronze Age settlement there. And the Romans dug for lead over there. There are old pack trails, Elizabethan houses, Georgian terraces in Lissom. This place has always been inhabited. Sometimes when work is hard I come here to find peace. It's beautiful and I think about all the people who have gone before me.'

'You come to find peace only when work is hard?'

She knew what he meant at once. 'Just peace. When work is hard or when my...private life is hard. At one time I seemed to come here two or three times a week.'

'I see. So is it your personal or your work life that is troubled at the moment?'

'Both,' she said. 'Look, there's a seat there, we can sit and be calm for a moment. If you want.'

'I want,' he said, after a pause.

She closed her eyes as she sat by him, wondered if it would be a good idea to reach for his hand. Perhaps not. That would complicate things far too much.

After a while she said, 'I want you to try to understand my point of view about these talks I've been asked to give. I know it's not what you think, but they are my ideas and honestly felt. I know what you feel for Johanne. I'm very fond of her myself and I want to do the best for her. We may disagree about talks on contraception but I need you to recognise my honesty. Remember I have a daughter myself. In another ten or eleven years I'll be going through what you're going through.'

He nodded. Then he asked a question that startled her. 'D'you think we fight over Johanne to stop us thinking about each other?'

This was a new idea and it rather alarmed her. But she had to consider it. 'Possibly,' she said after a while. 'Adam, I like…I like you a lot. I like working with you. And you showed me happiness on holiday that I…I had never dreamed of. But it had to be for a short time only.'

'Did it? Why?'

'I've told you why. Now, can we talk about contraception?'

'I wish I'd never heard the word. I certainly don't want to fight with you over it.' Then he turned to her and smiled and said, 'Well, only insofar as it affects people other than us.'

She punched him playfully. Now she knew things were going to be all right. 'It's important,' she said.

'True. Amy, I want to ask your advice. About Johanne.'

'Will you take it?' she asked.

'Who can tell? Certainly I can't make up my own mind. The thing is, Johanne's mother—my ex-wife—has resurfaced. She didn't write to me, she wrote straight to Johanne. She's visiting Leeds, something to do with a big shop opening. She wants to take Johanne out for the day. Johanne, of course, wants to go. I don't want her to.'

Amy's heart went out to him. She could see what he was suffering. 'D'you think your ex-wife is reconsidering? She now wants to be part of Johanne's life?'

'I doubt it very much. The man she's married to has made his position very clear. Now she's just playing with us.'

Amy looked at the hurt in his eyes and thought. 'If you think the woman's just playing with you, let Johanne go. I suspect your daughter has more sense than you're allowing for. She'll quickly see what is happening.'

'I'd love to think so.'

'Look, if you don't let her go she's going to hold it against you. Even if she has a great time, she's going to feel rejected afterwards, when her mother leaves.'

'I suppose so. And it's only for a day. Now, if it was a son I could—'

'Adam Ross! You say what I think you're going to say and you'll drive me screaming mad! You have a gorgeous daughter. So be grateful!'

'I am grateful,' he said. 'Of course she can go.'

She saw him again next morning in the surgery. He waved a brochure at her, which he'd taken out of the rack of health pamphlets that was kept in Reception. 'Amy! Have you ever been here?'

She looked at what he was holding. It was a description of a newly opened swimming bath in a town about fifteen miles away. 'Looks good,' she said, 'a sun area with palm trees, slides for the kids and an Olympic-sized pool for serious swimmers. No. I've never been.'

'I haven't managed any swimming for quite a while. Fancy bringing Elizabeth and coming with me this Saturday morning?'

Amy thought a moment. 'Johanne coming as well?'

'No, there's something on at school.' He turned and pointed at the grey skies outside. 'I thought it might be fun to remember what the Mediterranean was like.'

'I remember what the Mediterranean was like very well,' she told him, and blushed slightly when she saw the knowing smile on his lips. 'But Elizabeth would love it, and she'd certainly love being with you. Anyway, who d'you want to go with most? Me or Elizabeth?'

'I think the two of you are a perfect partnership,' he said smoothly. 'I only wish you were as easy to…cajole as Elizabeth.'

'I'll give you cajole! All right, then, say half past nine on Saturday?'

'Looking forward to it. Shall I pick you up at your house?'

'We'll be waiting outside,' she told him.

When he had gone, she wondered why she had agreed so readily. Her first intention when he arrived in Lissom had been to have as little to do with him as possible. But surely there was no harm in what she was doing? A visit for tea with Elizabeth and Johanne, now a morning trip to a swimming bath. It was all perfectly all right. Apart from that first kiss when he had called at her house, he had been nothing more to her than a friend.

But she had enjoyed the kiss.

Perhaps this was all part of a plan. He was trying to make her see that he was dependable, reasonable, not at all like her ex-husband. And he was succeeding. But the thought of her ex-husband made her remember. She'd been gravely wrong in her judgement of a man before. She could be wrong again.

It was a super swimming bath. If Adam and Amy didn't think so, Elizabeth certainly did. It was almost like being abroad again. The pool was free form, there was a variety of slides to drop into it—though Elizabeth had to be accompanied down the biggest slide. There was a big poolside area where you could buy drinks and sit and watch. And it was illuminated by artificial sunshine. Outside was a grey Derbyshire day. Here inside they could have been by the pool in the Mediterranean.

Elizabeth had never forgotten her big fish ride, so once again Adam had to swim around the pool with her riding on his back. He seemed to enjoy it quite as much as she did. There was a definite bond growing between the two and Amy wondered if it was altogether a good idea. She didn't want Elizabeth having something she couldn't have. Or could she? She and Elizabeth were a package. If you took one, you took both. Amy decided not to think further about this.

They swam for a while, tried all the slides and then Adam took her for a coffee by the poolside while Elizabeth splashed in the babies' pool. It was rather nice sitting there in their costumes. It was very nice sitting opposite Adam, as lean and as muscled as he had always been. Amy noticed him getting the odd admiring or appraising glance from passing women, and felt rather pleased that he was with her.

'We've had a few weeks,' he said after a while. 'You're getting used to having me around, you can see and talk to me without embarrassment. I've done as I said, I haven't harassed you. So now can we talk? Talk about us, that is.'

'I'm easier with you,' she admitted. 'I like being with you and sometimes I get such happy memories of you that… But perhaps memories are my problem. Still, we can talk. But you must start.'

There was a biscuit with his coffee. He carefully unwrapped it, broke it into four small pieces then put one piece into his mouth. Amy guessed that he was trying to be exact, trying to work out just what he needed to say to her. It was one of the rare occasions that she had seen him at a loss for words.

But then he started, 'We were having a holiday romance. It was coming to an end, only three days left. And then we would have had to decide on how we said goodbye to each other, what if anything there was for us in the future. We couldn't just part, could we?'

She had never thought of this. But there was only one obvious answer. 'No, perhaps not,' she said quietly.

'I know that your mother was ill, and it was the right thing to do to go back at once. It was an emergency. But it stopped you thinking about us, didn't it? You had something else to worry about so you didn't have to make any decisions.'

She was silent for a while. What he said could well be true—perhaps she had used her mother's illness as some kind of excuse. But still… 'We agreed from the start that this was something that would only last a while,' she said. 'That's what I wanted—I needed. I didn't want any long-term commitment.' With a small show of bravado she added, 'I still don't want any commitment.' Then she had to spoil it by adding, 'At least, I don't think so.'

He didn't pick up on this last comment, which surprised her. Instead, he seemed to talk about something different.

'You know I've been in Canada for a few weeks with my brother? My brother James? I've got a few photographs, you might like to see them. He's a geologist out there, got a wife Penny and a couple of tearaway kids. I'd like you to meet them someday.'

'Sounds nice,' said Amy, not knowing where the conversation was going.

'Penny is a geologist, too. She met James at a geologists' conference in England, she'd flown over specially to attend it. Anyway, they met, they had a lot in common and they seemed to like each other. But as far as I know, they didn't sleep together.'

'So it doesn't run in the family,' Amy said drily.

He grinned at her. 'We can joke about it. That's good.'

'Anyway, James was working in Aberdeen, Penny was working on the west coast of Canada. They exchanged e-mail addresses, intended to keep in touch. But after a week James thought he'd had enough of communicating by e-mail, so he took a fortnight's holiday and flew out to Vancouver. He didn't tell her he was coming, just surprised her. He told her that e-mailing wasn't enough, she was too important to him for that. So they had a fortnight together and when he flew back she had an engagement ring on her finger. They were married—in Canada—three months later and they're the happiest couple I know.'

'It's a great story,' said Amy. 'Just one thing. Had either of them been married before?'

'No. They got it right first time. It is possible, Amy. It might even be possible the second time. If you take the chance.'

'If you take the chance,' she said.

'Mummy, you said I could have an ice cream. Can I have a pink one with fruit on top?'

This was the end of any chance of serious conversation. But Adam didn't seem to mind. He fetched the required ice cream and then said to Amy, 'You will think about what I've said, won't you?'

'I'll think,' she promised.

She didn't have much chance to see anything of Adam over the rest of the weekend and when she went back to work on Monday they both seemed to be busy. He didn't ring her at home, as he had promised. She noticed this, thought the better of him. He would stick to what he had agreed.

But on Thursday they met at the surgery and he said, apparently carelessly, 'I'm going out for lunch at the pub round the corner. Fancy coming? We could chat a bit and—'

Her mobile phone rang. The voice on the other end sounded anxious. 'Amy? It's Alan Dunnings, Top Cliff Farm. I'm a bit worried about Dad. He's not been too bad recently, taking things easy, doing what you said. But this morning he was on his walk when he came across a cast sheep. Of course he had to wrestle it over, didn't he? And now he's sitting by the fire, and I don't like his colour and he's got pains in his chest.'

'Send for an ambulance,' said Amy. 'This could be serious.'

'It'll be more serious if I do. He hated it last time, he'll fight before he gets into an ambulance.'

'Look, I'll come up and see him now,' said Amy. 'But if he gets worse, send for that ambulance anyway.'

'Right, Amy. And thanks.'

She noticed that Adam had looked up when she'd said 'ambulance', now he asked, 'Was that one of your patients?'

'Dr Wright's patient really. They're old friends. Alf had a heart attack some weeks ago.' Quickly, she outlined the case to Adam.

'I see. You're going up to see him. Would you like me to come as well?'

'I'd like nothing better. Perhaps you can talk some sense into him.'

Alf Dunnings was sitting in his usual chair, his face grey, when they arrived. But he managed to smile when he saw Amy and was polite when introduced to Adam.

Adam took his pulse and blood pressure. Carefully, he listened to Alf's heart. Then he said, 'I'm sorry Alf, but Amy and your son are right. You have to go to hospital. Just for a day or two. We'll do some tests and then—'

'I'm not going to hospital! I can't breathe there. People die in hospitals.'

'Alf, you'll die yourself if...'

Amy had listened to this conversation, now she took Adam's arm and said, 'Could I have a word, Adam, please?'

Adam looked at her, obviously rather irritated at being interrupted when he was speaking to a patient. But he followed Amy to the other side of the room and said, 'You have something to add?'

'Tell him you're not sending him to hospital,' Amy said. 'Then come outside and we'll have a look around the farmyard with Alan.'

'But he needs to go to hospital! His son knows that, you said so, too. He just can't keep up that heart rate. And there's arrhythmia, too.'

'You can increase his dosage. I've got the pills with me. But for now just tell him he's not going to hospital. You can always change your mind in ten minutes.'

Adam looked at her searchingly, then walked over to Alf and said, 'For the moment you stay here. No hospital. But you do everything we tell you and we'll be up to see you again tomorrow.'

'OK,' said Alf.

Amy dragged Adam out to look around the farmyard and to chat with Alan. After a quarter of an hour they went back into the kitchen and Amy said, 'Dr Ross just wants another quick listen to your chest, Alf. Then we'll be off.'

Adam took out his stethoscope again, placed it on Alf's chest. After a while he looked up at Amy, arched his eyebrows. He was obviously surprised.

'As the doctor said, we'll be back to see you tomorrow, Alf,' Amy said. 'And until then, behave!'

'I will,' Alf said.

'It's called the no-hospital treatment,' Amy said as they bumped down the track away from High Clough Farm. 'Alf is terrified of hospital, he hated it when he was taken there after his first heart attack. So when he thought you were going to send him away, naturally his heart rate went up.'

'Naturally,' said Adam.

'And it came down to acceptable levels when he thought he wasn't having to leave the farm.'

'Illogical but understandable. Do you get many cases where the patient just won't accept what is best for them? Where they can't even see where they are going wrong?'

'Oh, plenty of cases. Sometimes even the most intelligent...' Her voice trailed away. 'You're not talking about patients, are you?'

'Not really. I'm talking about you.'

They turned into the main road, but she didn't drive quite as fast as usual.

'I've thought about what you said, Adam,' she told him. 'I've thought a lot. They say the burned child fears the fire and it's true. Well, I've been burned and I'm still afraid.'

His voice was gentle. 'You can learn, Amy. Fear disappears in time.'

'It depends on how afraid you are.'

She turned into a layby and parked, for a moment watching the traffic hurtling past. Then she said, 'I never told you the full story before. I will now.' She wriggled in her seat, trying to be comfortable. 'Things had been really bad with my husband, but at least I had my job. Then I fell pregnant. Elizabeth's conception was an...an accident. He had been out drinking and came home demanding what he called his "rights".'

Amy could hear her voice quavering, tried to make

it firm again. 'He hated it when he found I was going to have a baby, he wanted me to have an abortion. And I refused. Then it got worse when he found he was to have a daughter. And this was the man who I could remember being so marvellous! Anyway, I had Elizabeth, things got even worse and I told him I was divorcing him. And you know the rest.'

He leaned over to kiss her on the cheek. 'That was then, Amy. Things can get better.'

'I know that, I know that! Knowing is one thing. But feeling is another. And I'm afraid. But, Adam, I'm trying!'

He said nothing more but handed her a handkerchief. She wiped her eyes, then started the car. 'We mustn't be too late back,' she said.

Saturday was the day Johanne's mother was coming to take her out. On the Friday Amy saw how irritated and upset Adam was. When they had a minute alone she tried to calm him down. 'This is a bit of a test,' she said. 'It'll show how well you've brought up your daughter. And I think you'll pass the test. If what you say about them both is true, Johanne will enjoy her day but still come back to you happily.'

'I hope so,' he said. 'But I'm not very happy, and not too confident either. With that woman, things always go wrong.'

'Just wait and see.' Amy was hopeful.

She spent most of Saturday with her mother, trying to extract details from her about Noel. Her mother was irritatingly complacent, and refused to say anything except that she was happy. And Amy knew this to be true. Her mother looked younger, there was a glow about her. Amy was so pleased for her mother. If this was what love could do…but for other people.

Sunday morning at home was always something a bit different and special. Amy stayed in bed and Elizabeth came in with her. They giggled and bounced about and then Amy fetched them breakfast in bed. They sat side by side, eating it.

The phone rang, but it was a while before Amy could disentangle herself from her daughter and the sheets. Then she caught her breath, half with excitement, half with surprise. It was Adam. 'Hi, Adam! Sorry to be so long in replying. I was bouncing on the bed with Elizabeth.'

'It's good to have fun with your daughter. Sorry to ring you at home when I know you don't want me to.' She realised his tone was tired, even disillusioned.

'Is there anything wrong? How did yesterday go?'

'Johanne had a wonderful time. She came back with her face plastered with make-up, a new dress, dyed hair in a totally unsuitable style. She's fourteen, not twenty.'

Amy felt her morning was ruined, but she was not going to show this. 'Adam, did you phone just to take your bad temper out on me?'

'I'm sorry, Amy. Could we meet for a while? Not your place or mine, somewhere neutral.'

'Neutral? As in a war?' She looked out of the window, the weather was fine but crisp. 'All right,' she said. 'I'll put Elizabeth in her buggy. We'll go to the park by the river. I'll bring some bread for the ducks and we'll be there in about an hour. But, Adam, why are you—'

'In an hour.' He rang off.

Amy went back to play with Elizabeth, but it wasn't fun any more. At first she had been shocked at Adam's attitude. But now a slow anger began to burn inside her, getting hotter by the minute. She wasn't used to be spoken to in that way. She wasn't going to have it either. If Adam wanted a fight—for whatever reason—then he would find that she would give him one.

She dressed Elizabeth and herself warmly, got a stale half loaf and set off for the park. It was a lovely day again, with the leaves golden brown and the clearness of autumn. Once in the park Elizabeth had to get out of the buggy, to run along the path, kicking the piles of leaves with a swishing sound. She at least was happy.

Amy saw Adam waiting by the river, in jeans and a black leather jacket. He looked good. He had his back to her and was staring at the wooded hills above the town. It thrilled her just to see him—it always did. But this time it made her even more angry with herself.

He didn't hear her approach.

'Ducks!' shouted Elizabeth. 'Hello, Uncle Adam, I've got bread for the ducks.'

Adam turned to them. His face was stern at first, but he had to smile at Elizabeth. He picked her up, hugged her.

'First things first,' said Amy. 'We have to feed the ducks.'

'Of course. Being a parent is all-important.'

He stood to one side while Amy and Elizabeth threw in their bread, watching the ducks swoop and dive after the food. Elizabeth loved it. But eventually they were finished, and Amy buckled her into her buggy and gave her a teddy to cuddle.

She sat on a nearby bench and said, 'If we're going to talk, you can sit down.'

He sat on the far side of the bench from her and she went on, 'It's beautiful out now. Elizabeth and I would have loved to come out and meet you, to go for a quiet friendly walk in the park. But it's not going to be like that, is it?'

For a moment his bleak expression slipped and she thought she saw misery in his eyes. But then it hardened and he said, 'Probably not. How long have you known that my daughter was seeing a boy nearly three years older than her?'

Amy flinched, she could do without this. But she said, 'I've met them once, by chance. Near the entrance of that park by the school.'

'And they were doing what?'

'He was kissing her.'

'And how was he kissing her?'

Now Amy was getting angry. 'I got it wrong when I said he was kissing her. They were kissing each other. And they were kissing like any two teenagers who think they're in love.'

'Love! At fourteen? I know Johanne asked you not to tell me about them, but you didn't have to do what she wanted. Didn't you think I ought to know? Aren't I to be trusted with the welfare of my own daughter?'

Amy's shoulders slumped. She had no real answer. 'It was hard for me. I did what I thought best.'

'Quite so. And I find out about it from my ex-wife, who took great pleasure in telling me. Johanne had told her in confidence, but Angela thought I ought to know. I felt a fool and I felt betrayed.'

'Adam, I'm sorry.'

He shrugged. 'Well, it's done now. Johanne and I have sorted out some kind of pattern of living together. I see no reason why it should not work. But I feel let down by you. I thought I could trust you.'

'So did Johanne. I'm sorry, Adam. I did what I thought best.'

'Quite so. But I think it best in future if you only see Johanne when she's with me. And if you see her with any—'

'If I see her in any situation that seems dangerous to me, I'll tell you. But what is dangerous will be my decision.'

What was best to do both for Adam and herself? She wanted to discuss, to be reasonable, to see if there was something on which they could both agree. But when she looked at that hard-as-teak face, she knew there was no point. Adam had made up his mind. That was enough.

'I can only say that I won't try to get in touch with Johanne without telling you,' she said.

'Fine. I'll have to settle for that. Good morning.' And he walked away.

It wasn't very cold out but Amy felt as if her face was frozen. Quickly, she pushed Elizabeth home, in spite of her demands to feed the ducks again. Then she sat on her couch and burst into tears.

The following week was a nightmare. Amy carried on at work, realised that Adam was trying to see as little of her as possible. When they did meet, he smiled politely but distantly. She smiled politely back. And it hurt.

Ever ready for a little friendly gossip, Rita whispered to Amy, 'Dr Ross hasn't been himself all week. Really distant. You know his ex-wife came back to see him last Saturday? Perhaps he's missing her.'

'That right?' Amy asked, trying to put on a face of indifference. 'I can't say I've noticed, myself.'

She didn't know whether things were made better or worse when Dr Wright called a five-minute lunch meeting and told everyone that there was no longer any question of Amy being asked to talk about contraception in school. 'All the local schools have got together and have appointed a specialist speaker to do this work. The headmistress phoned me, saying that it was out of her hands now. She would have preferred Amy—and hopes that Amy will still come to give her ordinary talks.'

Amy glanced at Adam. As so often these days, his expression was unreadable.

She was missing passing the time of day with him. And she realised that his plan had been working. She had been getting to know him, to like him. In time perhaps they might have… But it was too late now.

On the Friday evening, when she was picking up Elizabeth from her mother's, Sylvia said, 'Can you come to tea tomorrow night? About six?'

Amy looked at her mother, rather surprised. 'A bit formal, isn't it?' she asked. The two of them were always dropping on and out of each other's houses.

'This is different. I want you to meet…well, I want you to meet Noel.'

Amy had her first real laugh in ages. 'You want

me to meet your boyfriend,' she said. 'You're anxious, hope that he'll make a good impression. Ma, this is the wrong way round. It's daughters who worry about introducing boyfriends to their mothers.'

'He wants to meet you,' her mother said, going rather pink. 'He's seen you at a distance and he wants to meet Elizabeth, too.'

'That's nice. I'm looking forward to meeting him.' Amy just couldn't help herself. 'It's good to see you getting out and about,' she said. 'Have you...you know what yet?'

Now her mother turned scarlet. But then she laughed. 'I'm your mother,' she said. 'Just keep quiet.'

'Looking forward to meeting him,' said Amy.

When they met, she really liked Noel. He arrived with flowers for her mother, a smaller bunch for her and a teddy for Elizabeth. Amy realised that he had thought of it all himself—he had not been prompted by her mother. They had a pleasant meal together and then Amy took Elizabeth home. At the door she whispered to her mother, 'Now, if you can't be good, be careful.' And her mother blushed again.

At home Amy bathed Elizabeth and put her to bed. Then she sat on her couch by the fire and felt just a little depressed. She was so happy to see her mother happy. But it made her wonder—was she missing something herself? Why couldn't she have a love life of her own?

It was five days later. She was kept out late—one of her independent old ladies who lived on her own had fallen and was distressed. And she refused to go to hospital. Amy phoned the lady's daughter who said she would come round and stay the night, but couldn't arrive for another hour or so. So Amy waited until the daughter arrived.

In due course, Amy went to pick up Elizabeth.

It was an evil night. It had rained all day and now the wind was growing, rattling the raindrops on the windscreen. There were few people out, the streets of Lissom almost deserted.

That was why Amy noticed one figure. A girl in a dark mac, carrying a heavy bag, head down as she walked towards the bus station. It was Johanne.

Amy remembered what she had promised Adam. But surely he wouldn't object if she gave his daughter a lift in this weather. The next question was, did Amy want to get involved in the family again? Well, yes, she did. Just a bit.

She pulled over, reached and opened the passenger door. 'Get in, Johanne. I'll give you a lift.'

'Amy, what are you—?'

'Come on, get in,' Amy said impatiently. 'You'll get us both wet. Where are you going?'

Johanne climbed in, wedged her bag on her knees. 'If you could drop me off at the bus station,' she said, 'that'd be great.'

Amy remembered that Adam was working at the surgery until eight that night. It was now seven. Lightly, she asked, 'Where are you going on this evil night, Johanne?'

There was no answer. Amy stopped the car, turned on the overhead light and looked at Johanne's grim, rain-streaked face. 'Come on, Johanne. Where are you going?'

'I'm going to my mother's.'

'And is she expecting you?'

'No. But I am her daughter.'

Amy tried to keep her voice casual. 'Does your dad know you're going?'

'No, he doesn't. But he doesn't have to worry. I've left him a letter.'

'I see. May I ask why you're going?'

'You know very well!' Johanne said, her voice rising. 'He won't let me see Jack, he's on at me all the time, telling me to work. And I do work. My project was the best in the class. And he won't let me see you. I can't stand it and I'm leaving!' Now she was nearly in tears.

Amy sighed. This was the last thing she wanted. 'Can I persuade you to go back, Johanne? You know he loves you. Perhaps if you talk to him—'

'I've tried talking! He doesn't listen. And now you're going to tell him that you've met me, aren't you? It doesn't matter—he can't lock me up all the time.'

'Of course I'm going to tell him,' Amy said. 'He'll worry and he'll tell the police.'

'Police?' Johanne obviously hadn't thought of this.

'You're an under age runaway,' said Amy.

Amy thought for a minute and then made a decision. Things were bad between Adam and herself. What did it matter if she made them worse? 'I've got an idea,' she said. 'Would you like to stay with me and Elizabeth for a couple of weeks?'

Johanne looked at her with surprise and hope in her face. 'Could I? Oh, Amy, I'd love that and I could still see Jack and I'd help and—'

'I've got to make your dad accept. But for now, come home and get dry.'

Johanne leaned over and kissed her on the cheek, and Amy felt the wet hair brush against her face. 'Amy, you're wonderful!'

'Let's hope your father thinks so,' Amy muttered. She was wondering how this would affect her relationship with Adam. After this, would there be any relationship?

She took Johanne home, told her to have a bath and then change out of her wet clothes. 'This is the spare bedroom,' she said. 'It's a bit bare and a bit cluttered with junk.'

'It's wonderful,' said Johanne. 'I can be happy here. I do hope you can put things all right with Dad.'

'So do I,' Amy said feelingly.

Amy phoned her mother, who was happy to keep Elizabeth overnight. Then she phoned the surgery. Rita was on duty. 'Tell Dr Ross not to go home,' Amy said. 'There's a matter I have to discuss with him urgently. I'll be waiting for him when he finishes.'

'He usually likes to get home to his daughter.'

'He can spare me five minutes,' said Amy.

It was still raining when she drove into the surgery car park and ran into Reception. Adam had been given the message and came out of his consulting room a couple of minutes later. He looked quite concerned, there was none of the dislike he had shown recently.

'Hello, Amy. Terrible night to pull you out. You should be sitting in front of the fire with Elizabeth.'

Just my luck, Amy thought. He's trying to be nice and I'm going to make him really angry. She said, 'This is not surgery business, I don't want to talk here. A few days ago you arranged to meet me to talk about Johanne. Now I'm doing the same. Where can we talk?'

His face was impassive. 'I'm not sure I like the sound of this,' he said. 'Are you interfering?'

'There's a pub down the road, the Cross Keys. It's pleasant and quiet, we can talk there, just for ten minutes.'

She still couldn't read his expression. But eventually he said, 'All right, then, the Cross Keys, just for ten minutes. I'll just phone Johanne and tell her I'll be late.'

Amy took a breath and said, 'There's no point. She's not at home, she's at my house. Now, the Cross Keys?'

Now his face did show what he was feeling. He was blazingly angry. Amy quailed at his expression, but she had to go on now. 'This had better be good,' he whispered, 'but I'll see you there.'

It was an unpleasant night and still early so there were few people in the pub. They had the snug to themselves. Adam asked her what she wanted and fetched a glass of red wine for her, half a pint of bitter for himself. He seemed composed, but she could see the anger underneath. 'Now, what about my daughter?' he said eventually.

Amy tried to tell him.

'So Johanne is deeply unhappy? She's tried to run away from home and just by luck you found her?'

'Otherwise she might have been on the bus, going to your ex-wife.'

He winced. 'You invited her to stay for an indeterminate time?'

'I told her I'd ask you.'

'Will you encourage her to see this older boy?'

'I shall neither encourage nor discourage her. If she wants, she can invite him home for tea and I'll make him welcome. And there will be definite ground rules about how long she can stay out and where she can go to.'

'I see. I need to think.' He sat in silence and once again she had no idea what he was thinking. She fetched herself a tonic water, another half pint for him.

Eventually he said, 'Amy, I'd be very pleased if Johanne could stay with you for a week or so. Then we can think again. She'll go to school as usual?'

'Of course.'

'She has a key, she can fetch what she needs from the flat tomorrow. Of course, I shall pay you—'

'Adam! I've kept calm so far because we both have to. But now you're making me angry. Johanne will be my guest.'

'I'm sorry. And, believe me or not, I'm grateful. Yes. Of course Johanne can stay with you.' He finished his beer in one swallow. 'You'll…look after her?'

'As best I can,' Amy said simply. 'By the way, there's a letter waiting for you. Things have changed since she wrote it. Why don't you keep it unopened, ask her when you see her again if she wants you to open it?'

'Good idea. Now, I think I'd better be off.' He stood, his smile a grimace. 'My flat will seem lonely without her.'

Amy could feel his pain.

Amy felt emotionally exhausted when she got home. But she picked up a little when she saw how delighted Johanne was when she heard her father had said that she could stay with Amy. She was more pleased when she saw that Johanne felt sorry for her father—and was hopeful that he wouldn't open the letter that she had left.

It took a couple of days for Johanne to settle in, but very soon she was a member of the family, equally at home with Sylvia and Elizabeth. Amy felt happy, too. But there was still an anxiety that she couldn't stifle. She knew this situation couldn't go on.

Johanne was playing with Elizabeth one evening when Sylvia took Amy to one side. With a smile she said, 'You embarrassed me the other day, asking me about Noel. Now I'm going to do the same to you. Exactly what is between you and Adam?'

'Nothing!' Amy said forcefully, then looked at her mother's sardonic face. 'Oh, all right, then, I'll tell you. We had an affair when I was on holiday. A holiday romance. Now he wants more—he wants to get serious.'

'And what do you want?'

'I'm afraid, Ma. After being married to Paul, I'm afraid.'

'I was afraid of being so close to Noel,' her mother said. 'For that matter, he was afraid, too. But we're getting there.'

'Good. But you were happily married and I gather that he was, too. Look what I went through.'

'All life's a risk,' her mother said. 'You just can't avoid it.'

Amy's relationship with Adam was odd. Every day she reported to him that Johanne was all right. He had lost his previous hostility and now was concerned and friendly. But his concern was for Johanne. It was as if the two of them were brought together by a joint interest in his daughter, and whatever personal feelings they might have had been put on hold.

Amy was pleased with this. She saw him regularly but she wasn't too involved. It gave her a breathing space.

After a week Amy asked Johanne if she wanted to go home, and Johanne said no. If Amy didn't mind, and if it wasn't too much trouble, she'd like to stay. Amy reported this to Adam.

She could tell he wasn't pleased. He wasn't angry so much as hurt. Well, having children could be a hurtful process. He said, 'If you don't mind having her, I'm…glad that she's found a friend. But there's now one condition. Please, don't be insulted but I must pay you something.' He managed a small grin. 'Since she left, my food bill has halved. I never realised how much I had been spending on junk food.'

'You can give me something towards her food,' Amy said, 'but I'm not looking to make a profit.' She took a breath and then said, 'Perhaps I should tell you, Jack Collis is coming to tea on Saturday evening. Johanne says she's going to cook.'

'Heaven help the poor lad,' said Adam. Amy smiled.

CHAPTER SEVEN

IT WAS the following Wednesday that Amy took the next step. By chance she met Adam in the surgery car park. He smiled at her, which was a good sign. 'Adam, I've got something to ask you. I'm giving a dinner party on Saturday night. Elizabeth will be there, and my mother and her new friend Noel are invited. Johanne is inviting Jack. And I'd like you to come.'

She looked at his face, hoping for some sign of what he wanted to do. But all she got was that blank look she had seen too often that meant that he was thinking.

'So I am to meet the young man in question. On neutral ground.'

'You'll both be my guests. And I know you both well enough to know that you'll both act properly.'

'So you know—Jack is his name, isn't it?'

'It is, as you well know. And, yes, I've met him two or three times. He's well-mannered, a bit shy. I think he's genuinely fond of Johanne.'

'Fond of?'

'I think he has a genuine regard for her,' Amy said firmly. 'And, in fact, I know the family. They sell agricultural goods, an old-established, well-thought-of firm.'

'You know what you're asking me to do? Meeting this young man means that I approve of the relationship. That I admit that everything I've said to my daughter is wrong.'

'I'd say that friendship is a better word than relationship. And what I'm asking you to do is help your daughter. And perhaps yourself.'

He hunched his shoulders, as if to ward off a punch. Then he said, 'Thank you for your invitation. I'd like to accept.'

'Good. I'm calling this a dinner, but Ma and Noel are going on to a lecture on local history afterwards and Johanne and Jack are going to the school dance. So it won't be for all the evening.'

'Fair enough. What shall I wear?'

'Smart casual will be fine.'

She bit her lip. She had nerved herself to ask this next question but she didn't know what kind of answer she might get. 'You're a good-looking man, Adam, you turn women's heads. I bet you were a good-looking boy. Just how old were you when you kissed a girl—seriously—for the first time?'

There was a long pause and then he said, flatly, 'Thirteen. How old were you when you were first kissed?'

'Thirteen,' she said.

The meal was to be a joint endeavour between three women and they started to prepare it at lunchtime on Saturday. Elizabeth recognised that something exciting was going to happen, so she had to join in.

With the meal being prepared beforehand, serving it would be just a matter of fetching dishes from the kitchen. Amy had decided to have a starter of dressed salad with smoked fish, a main course of a big bowl of rice with kebabs of beef, pork and chicken, with sauces to the side, and a dessert of fresh fruit with whipped cream.

The cooking was finished in plenty of time, the kitchen cleared, the table laid. Then the three women—and Elizabeth—took turns in the bathroom then changed.

Amy lent Johanne one of her long skirts, it went well with a blouse bought in Palma.

Once again Amy put on the lacy underwear she hadn't worn since the holiday and a dress she hadn't worn since then. Only when she had it on did she realise that it was the dress she had worn the night after she had slept with Adam for the first time. Would he remember? The evening after the storm, when they'd had to sit and pretend that nothing very much had happened. Perhaps he would think that wearing it was some kind of message. Whatever, she thought she looked nice in it.

Then the four of them were ready.

'We can sit down and relax now,' said Sylvia.

There was a rattle at the door, a whooshing sound and it started to rain. Not just any rain but a Derbyshire downpour.

'Jack'll get wet through,' said Johanne. 'He's not allowed to drive yet, though he's learning.'

Noel was the first to arrive, smiling, with flowers and a bottle of wine. Amy noted the way he looked at her mother, kissed her. She wanted someone to look at her like that. Or did she? She remembered Adam had offered—in effect.

The next one to arrive was Adam. Amy saw his car draw up outside. She said to Johanne, 'It's your dad. Do you want to let him in?' She knew Johanne hadn't seen him for a fortnight, though they had phoned. Johanne paled, but went to the front door.

Amy saw Adam kiss his daughter, heard him say, 'You look very nice in that outfit.' Johanne said nothing, but hugged him.

Adam came in, kissed Amy on the cheek and presented her with more flowers. He said, 'And you, too, look well in that dress. I think I remember it.' Amy blushed, then introduced him to Noel. The two men seemed to get on at once.

One guest to come, Amy thought desperately. He's not late, the first two were early. I hope things go all right. As if guessing her thoughts, Johanne said, 'Jack's going to get awfully wet. He will come, won't he, Amy?'

Amy could hear the desolation in her voice, and said, 'Of course he'll come.'

Then they both saw a large Land Rover appear outside. Two people got out of it and hurried to the porch with their heads bent under a large golfing umbrella. Amy decided she should open the door. There, looking smart in a grey suit and with a slightly apprehensive expression, was Jack. With him was an older man, also blond, with a cheerful, smiling face. 'Hi! I'm Harry Collis,' he said, extending a hand. 'I brought Jack because it was raining, and I just wanted to say hello and thanks for inviting him.'

'Come inside and say hello to everyone,' Amy said instantly.

Harry hesitated. 'I'd like that,' he said. 'But I have to go straight off afterwards.'

Amy watched as he shook hands with Adam. It was

quite fascinating, the two men seemed to like each other at once. But there was no time for a long chat. Harry had to go. Then Johanne nerved herself and said, 'This is Jack, Dad. My...friend.'

Adam took the extended hand. 'I'm pleased to meet you at last,' he said. 'I've heard a lot about you.'

'Pleased to meet you, too,' said Jack.

'If you all like to sit down, we can start,' said Sylvia.

Amy thought it turned out to be a very pleasant meal. She could see the apprehension of both Johanne and Jack, but it slowly melted as Adam put himself out to be as welcoming as possible. Noel was also very good, having the solicitor's skill of redirecting a conversation if the subject became awkward. And everyone agreed, the cooking was wonderful.

So the dinner was a great success. Her mother and Noel left first, to go to their lecture.

Johanne said, 'Jack and I will have to go soon, but there's the dishes first and I—'

'Don't you dare mention dishes,' said Amy. 'Just go off and enjoy yourselves.'

Adam said, 'Johanne and Jack can't go out in this weather. I'll give them a lift in the car.'

Amy saw Johanne and Jack exchange glances, but there was nothing they could do. She said, pointing at a drooping Elizabeth, 'I've got to put sleepyhead here to bed.' Then, greatly daring, she said, 'If you want to come back for another coffee, Adam, you'll be welcome.'

He looked at her, she felt her face warm. He said, 'I'd like that very much.'

* * *

Elizabeth had really enjoyed herself, but now she was overexcited and it took quite a while to bathe her and calm her and get her into bed. Amy was only halfway through her bedtime story when the front doorbell rang. She ran downstairs, with her apron over her dress, to let Adam in. She gabbled, 'Sorry about the mess. Get yourself a coffee. I've just got to get Elizabeth to sleep so put the TV on if you want.' Then she rushed back upstairs, more concerned about her daughter than anything else.

Amy finished the story, saw she was asleep. A quick trip to the bathroom to pat cold water on her cheeks and put on a touch of lipstick. Then she went back downstairs.

At the beginning of the evening she had been apprehensive, but everything had gone better than she had expected. Now she was feeling apprehensive again. Why had she invited Adam back for coffee? The fact that she had wanted to invite him was really irrelevant.

He wasn't sitting in the living-room. And what had happened to the dinner dishes? The table had been cleared. She looked in the kitchen door and blinked. He was in his shirtsleeves, his tie loosened and an apron around his waist. A frilly one at that. The washing-up was done and neatly stacked, the food ready to be put in cupboards and fridge.

'You washed up!' she said, even though it was quite obvious.

'Well, you cooked and you were busy. It was the least I could do.'

'But guests don't wash up.'

'Perhaps I think I am a special guest,' he said cheerfully, 'the one invited to stay at the end. I liked that.'

She chose not to wonder if he was a special guest or not. 'Well, sit down now and I'll make fresh coffee,' she said. 'And I brought back some of that brandy we enjoyed in Spain. Would you like some?'

'I really would. It might bring back memories.' Then he grinned and said, 'If we're moving back into the living-room, I'll take the apron off.'

'I'll do the same in a minute. Now, go and sit down.'

She poured two brandies, percolated fresh coffee and fussed with a little plate of biscuits, all carefully arranged on a tray. Then she placed the tray on the coffee-table. He was sitting on the couch, she made to sit in an easy chair. 'If you sat by me it would be more friendly,' he said.

She hesitated. Then she came to sit by him on the couch. It was a small couch, only a two-seater, and he spread his arm over the back of it to make room for her.

She sat, and sighed. 'I just want to sit and drink my coffee and sip my brandy and be calm,' she said. 'I've been living on my nerves all day and I need a rest.'

'So you're all right now? Everything troublesome is over?'

'I think things have gone really well.' Then, with a frankness that embarrassed her, she said, 'But I'm still a bit on edge, sitting next to you on the couch.'

'You have nothing to fear from me,' he said softly. 'Lean back and relax.'

So she did. She felt a huge rush of fatigue, it was rather pleasant. She drank a little of her coffee, all of the brandy and leaned her head back on the couch. Inevitably, her eyes closed. It was comfortable there. She could feel the warmth of her fire, perhaps of the warmth of Adam's body. It didn't matter. She couldn't be bothered to think any more. All had gone well. She went to sleep. Her last drowsy memory was of the last time she had slept by his side, on the balcony in his hotel room. And even that didn't disturb her.

Consciousness returned slowly. She wasn't sure how long she had been asleep. But her body wasn't as it had been when she had dozed off. Now her head was firmly on Adam's shoulder. One of her arms was around his waist and his arm was holding her to him. Their bodies were touching, pressed together. She could smell his aftershave and the distant scent of his body. It was so comfortable there.

Too comfortable. She could end up wanting things she could not have. She jerked herself upright, found herself gazing into his smouldering grey eyes.

'You should rest more,' he said. 'I know how stressful today has been for you.'

She wasn't expecting sympathy, understanding. 'I can cope,' she said. She reached for her cup of now cold coffee and drained it. 'Adam, I've got to know now. What do you think of Jack? And of Johanne seeing him?'

She saw him think before answering, and her body tensed. 'I liked the boy,' he said eventually. 'He is well-mannered, knows enough not to talk when he's not sure of himself. He seemed genuinely fond of Johanne. And I liked his father as well.'

She felt the tension start to drain from her. 'So?' she queried. 'What'll be your attitude in the future?'

He sighed. 'I've lost my wife, Johanne is all I have. The thought of losing her is…hard.'

'She's not yours, she's now nearly her own person,' said Amy. 'She's not a child any more, though of course she's not yet an adult. It'll be hard but you just have to let her mature. Mature socially, intellectually, morally—and sexually. You can guide but you can't prescribe.'

He shook his head. 'My brain tells me that that's true. But my feelings tell me something else. I'll cope, Amy, and it's good of you to bother with me.' He thought for a minute and then said, 'Tell her that her letter is still unopened, she can have it back if she wants. And when she wants to come back home—or you want to get rid of her—I'll try to make things better.'

Now it was Amy's turn to be silent. After a while she said, 'Was it hard to say that?'

He smiled ruefully. 'Very hard. No one likes having to admit they've been wrong.'

'You've not been wrong! You've tried too hard and you've just been…not right. Oh, and we don't want to get rid of Johanne, she's like one of the family. I hope that when she eventually goes back to you, she'll visit us.'

'You can bet on it. We'll have to…'

He paused. Then with the arm that was still round her shoulders he pulled her to him and kissed her.

At first she was shocked. She tried to struggle. But

as she did so she realised that he wasn't holding her very hard, and she didn't really want him to stop. So he kissed her and she let him. He stroked her hair and she felt calm, relaxed, very happy.

It was only a gentle kiss and when he stopped she was content to lie there across his chest, held by his comforting arms. 'I liked that,' she said.

'So did I.'

His hand was moving up and down her back, soothing and yet exciting at the same time. He said, 'You know there were three couples here tonight, three generations. Noel and your mother, the oldest generation, seemed to have got things sorted out. So do Jack and Johanne, the youngest generation. It's only us two in the middle who can't get things right.'

'I don't want to talk any more,' she said. 'I'm too tired to think. But you can kiss me again if you like. You're being insidious again, aren't you?'

He kissed her, just as she had wanted, then he glanced at her clock. 'The school dance finishes at eleven o'clock,' he said. 'I told Jack and Johanne I'd pick them up and run them home. It's only a quarter to ten now and we—'

She giggled. 'Dr Ross, I can guess what you're thinking. But there are two objections. One, some good things should never be rushed. Two, for this feminine reason and that, it's just not really possible at the moment.'

There was a moment's sad silence, then he laughed. 'I think you're wonderful,' he said. 'You did say I could kiss you again?'

*   *   *

Adam caught Amy early on Monday afternoon, just before she left the surgery. She was alone in the coffee-room, about to pour herself a drink, when he came up behind her and kissed the back of her neck. It was a shock, but a delightful one.

'Adam! I work here, remember?'

'I remember. It's a wonderful thing, remembering. D'you remember dancing with me in the hotel grounds in the open air?'

She looked out of the window. It was a grey, bleak day, the wind chasing the leaves across the lawn outside. She shivered. 'I remember. Different then, wasn't it?'

'I like dancing and so do you,' he said.

'I do like it. But I don't get too much chance in Lissom.'

He smiled triumphantly. 'Ah. Fell for it, didn't you? Next Saturday is the Marquis's Charity Ball, I've just been told about it. I gather there's going to be a table for those of the staff here at the surgery who want to go. I'd like you to go with me.'

This was unexpected. Her initial reaction was of pleasure—she'd love to go. And with Adam.

'It's a big social event,' Amy acknowledged.

'You've been before?'

'Four years ago,' she said flatly, 'with my—with the man I was married to.'

'Ghosts. Get rid of them. Don't look back, look forward. Come with me to the ball.'

She was very tempted. She'd not been anywhere exciting since her holiday. Don't think about that! she told herself. But last time she had gone to the Marquis's Ball she had enjoyed dressing up, had enjoyed being with a party of friends. Don't kid your-self! she thought. You just want to go with Adam.

'I'd love to go with you,' she said, 'but we'll be part of the surgery party. We're just going to the dance together. This does not mark a change in our relationship.'

'Who could think such a thing?' he murmured.

Arrangements were easy to make. Elizabeth would stay the night with her grandmother and Johanne would stay there, too. She was now considered part of the family. Noel would come round for the eve-ning—he was there regularly. So that was sorted.

Amy found herself looking forward to the evening. She booked a hair appointment for Saturday after-noon. She couldn't really justify buying herself a new evening dress. Perhaps one of the dresses she had bought to go on holiday? Then she remembered something, and she went upstairs.

There was a closet behind the bathroom, where all the junk got pushed. Amy leaned inside, shoved away parcels and boxes and dragged out a trunk. It hadn't been opened for over two years.

For a moment she looked at the trunk and resisted the temptation to push it back in the closet. Then she blew away the dust and opened it. Inside was a flat cardboard box. She took it out, slammed the lid of the trunk shut and thrust it away. Then she wondered why she was making such a fuss.

Inside the box was a dress she had bought to wear to go out with her husband—in fact, to this very Marquis's Ball. He had always enjoyed social func-tions, said he enjoyed showing off his wife.

Sometimes she had felt like a trophy. And he had always drunk too much. Shortly after buying this dress their relationship had really fallen apart. And she had never worn the dress.

She thought of what Adam had said when he had invited her. 'Ghosts. Get rid of them!' Well, she would.

She tore at the sealing on the side of the box, pulled it open and pushed aside the layers of tissue paper. Then she lifted out the dress. It was made of a rich ivory silk. She ran her hand over the material—it felt so good. She was still in the upstairs hall and on impulse she stepped out of her jeans and pulled off her shirt. Then she slipped the dress over her head and went to look at herself in the bedroom mirror.

Hmm. Her hair was a mess. The sturdy bra she was wearing would have to go, but the dress itself…it made her look like a princess.

Carefully she took it off and laid it on the bed. This dress was too good to be ignored as a miserable memory of a husband who had abused her. She would wear it. She would lay ghosts, look forward in life.

By Saturday she was very excited. Johanne offered to stay to help her dress, but Amy didn't want her to know just how excited she was. She didn't want Johanne thinking too closely about her father and her going out together. So Johanne stayed happily with Sylvia.

Amy had a luxurious afternoon and evening. After her visit to the hairdresser's there was a long soak in a bath scented with oils. Then she sat in her dressing-gown, seeing to her nails. Then a body lotion, the lacy underwear again, the dress and then make-up. It had been a long time since she had spent so much time just pampering herself.

Finally she was finished, and went to survey herself in the long bedroom mirror. You look good, she told herself with pride.

She went downstairs and sat upright on her couch, waiting for Adam. Her heart was beating more strongly than usual. Tonight was going to be a night out of the normal run of her life but it would commit her to nothing.

The doorbell rang. When she let him in, he kissed her gently on the lips. He looked good, too. She had always thought that there were few things more flattering than evening dress for men. His was in a light-weight black silk, with a red rose buttonhole.

'You look sensational,' he said, as he surveyed the ivory dress. 'Really sensational. You don't need this, and I had to guess the colour anyway. But I wanted to buy you something.'

He presented her with a flower in a transparent box. It was an orchid, and when he pinned it to her shoulder she thought she looked better than ever. They looked at each other, thoughts unspoken.

Beforehand they had agreed to leave both cars behind, to travel there and back by taxi. 'I don't want to drink a vast amount,' he had told her. 'I just don't want to be counting every half-glassful.'

'I think that's very sensible.'

Then the doorbell rang again. It was the taxi. He kissed her again gently on the lips, and escorted her out.

*   *   *

The ball was held in the ballroom of the Marquis's ancestral home. The Marquis was there himself, greeting his guests, obviously pleased to see them. He was beaming, bald, the famous white moustache spreading over his face.

They were directed straight to the surgery table, met their friends there. She was going to enjoy the evening. Of course, she was one of a party of friends, and in no way did Adam indicate that she was more to him than just a friend and colleague. She danced with other men in the party, he danced with other women.

But he danced with her most, and he was the best dancer. He made her feel special.

And it was a special occasion. The tables were covered with white linen, there were complimentary bottles of champagne on hand, and waiters brought round little trays of delightful little titbits. It all made her so happy.

And, yes, Adam was undoubtedly the best dancer. She closed her eyes as they swayed around under the sparkling crystal chandeliers. 'What are you thinking?' he asked. 'I can always tell when you're thinking. And now you're frowning. Not a good evening to frown.'

'Just one thing. I'll say it once and then the subject is closed. I told you I was here four years ago with my ex-husband? I can remember it. Well, I'm much happier here with you.'

'That is good. And to copy you, I'm happier here with you than I have been for some time. I think we've both decided to live for the moment. This is a magic night. It even looks fairy tale. But at midnight you won't run off, leaving a glass slipper?'

'Not a chance. I'm staying here with Prince Charming. But I'll be back with the cinders and the nurse's blue uniform on Monday morning.'

His arm tightened around her and they danced on with no further words.

In time the ball drew to an end. For every lady there was a present, a little box wrapped in silver paper. Like all the others, Amy unwrapped hers at once. Inside the box was a tiny porcelain dragon. Amy remembered the dragon on the Marquis's coat of arms.

Then it was the end of the ball. The Marquis made a short speech, thanking everyone for coming and saying how much they had made for charity. 'The dragon is a symbol of hope. And I'd like to remind you of my family motto and recommend it to you as a way to live. "Live for Today, Hope for Tomorrow".'

'I'll keep my little dragon on my dressing-table,' Amy told Adam. 'It'll remind me of you—and of this night.'

'The night isn't finished yet,' he told her, and she wasn't quite sure why she shivered.

Their taxi arrived, he held her hand as they were driven home. Then, in a carefully neutral voice, he said, 'I shouldn't drive. The taxi is taking you home, I'll get it to drop me off afterwards.'

She said nothing for a while then said, 'I was rather hoping you'd come in for coffee. If you'd like to, that is.'

'I'd like to. Are you sure?'

'Very sure,' she said. There was firmness in her voice, she *was* very sure. In the hand that he didn't hold was clutched the little dragon. She remembered the Marquis's family motto. She would live for today, hope for tomorrow.

Her little house was warm as they walked in. She had left the two corner lights on, and it looked cosy and comfortable. 'Coffee won't be a moment,' she said. 'Why don't you take off your jacket and undo your tie? Be comfortable.'

She placed her dragon on the mantelpiece. 'He'll look after me,' she said.

In the kitchen she fumbled with kettle and percolator, not really knowing what she was doing. Eventually she arranged a tray as she had before, with coffee, biscuits, brandy and glasses. She took the tray through and saw that he had done as she had suggested and taken off his jacket and tie. She could see his broad shoulders, the strong column of his neck. He looked at her, his eyes unreadable.

She said, 'I can't sit on the couch in this dress, it's only suitable for upright chairs. I'm going to put on my robe.' She frowned. 'I've been groping in the kitchen, I think the zip is stuck at the back. Can you free it?'

She turned her back to him. His fingers reached down inside the neck of the dress, then there was the long buzz as the zip was eased down. He ran his finger from the nape of her neck to the strap of her bra. 'All done,' he whispered. She crossed her arms to hold the dress onto her front and ran upstairs.

In her bedroom she kicked off her shoes, then carefully took off the dress and hung it up. For a moment she was irresolute—but this was her home, she could do as she wished. She took off her tights. By accident she caught a glance of herself in her wispy white underwear, concealing so little. Her cheeks flushed. Then she grabbed her long blue robe from behind the door, belting it tightly. She pushed her feet into her slippers.

She turned off the main light, clicked on the much-loved Tiffany lamp on her dressing-table. It made her bedroom a place of mystery, of shaded colour, and she loved it. Then she went downstairs.

She sat by him on the couch, poured the brandy and the coffee. Desperately, she tried to start a light conversation. 'A lovely ball, wasn't it?' she asked.

'You said the right word before. It was magic. It was a fairy tale, and Cinderella invited me back. But there are no cinders here.'

His arm was around her. Deliberately he bent to kiss her. 'The Marquis told us,' he said, 'to live for today. So that's what we will do.'

His kiss seemed to last for ever. And when at last their lips parted she saw the glitter in his eyes and the warmth came to her cheeks. She knew so well what he was feeling, she was feeling it herself. Her voice faltered as she said, 'Drink your coffee and brandy. I want mine.'

They both drank, said nothing. There was a *ting* as they replaced their cups. Then he stood, took her two hands in his and lifted her to her feet. She felt that all decisions had been made and she was happy with them. Live for today.

She shuddered as he ran his hands up the sleeves

of her robe. His fingers met behind her neck, gently eased her towards him. There was the quickest, lightest of kisses then he moved back. His hands trailed down the front of her robe, came to rest on the tied belt. His expression was absorbed, intense, as if he could think of nothing else.

He undid the knot she had tied so tightly, opened her robe and eased it off her shoulders so it fell round her ankles. She breathed in, suddenly, sharply. Warmth spread through her body. It was almost impossible not to clasp her hands in front of her in the universal gesture of modesty. She had seen herself in the mirror, knew that her underwear didn't hide but accentuated her body. The scalloped edge of her lace half-bra emphasised the swell of her breasts. The high-cut briefs suggested what was underneath.

Now there was no mistaking the passion in his eyes. She knew what he wanted, could feel the desperation smouldering in him. And she needed it herself. He took her in his arms, his mouth came down on hers in a kiss almost brutal in its want.

She reacted at once, her mouth opening to his onslaught, taking him as he wished to take her. All of her body was responding to him. She could feel her nipples hardening, thrusting towards him. There was a warmth, almost a dampness between her legs. She knew she wanted, she needed him.

The tightness of his grip slackened. Instead of pulling her to him, his hands stroked her back, sending ripples of delight through her body. 'This isn't fair,' she managed to gasp. 'First, you're still dressed. And there's no hurry.'

She leaned back, unbuttoned his shirt. Then she

pulled it away from his chest. Her head stooped so she could kiss him there. Her tongue touched his nipples and she could tell from his groan just what delight it gave him.

Now she was determined, but at the edge of her mind she knew there was still something she had to say. 'We are living for now,' she told him fiercely. 'This is another holiday. There is no commitment, no promise. This is only now.'

'I know what I want now,' he whispered back. 'I want you.'

She took one of his hands in hers and led him upstairs. They went to her bedroom, stood facing each other. He removed her bra then, as she had done to him, bent to kiss her breasts, her nipples almost painful in their engorged intensity. She felt herself whimpering with delight and expectation.

Now his hands were on her hips, his fingertips under the elastic, sliding the flimsy fabric downwards. Then he brushed the springiness of the curls there, making her cry aloud with delight.

And he held her. For a minute or an hour, she did not know.

He threw back the duvet, gently laid her there. She saw him looking down at her naked body, the coloured glass of her Tiffany lamp making her glow deep blue, rich green—odd but somehow exciting.

He stepped back, there was the rustle of his clothes. The bed dipped as he leaned beside her. 'We have all the time in the world,' he said. 'We must enjoy each other.'

'We have tonight and that is all that I care about,'

she said. 'Now you lie there, lie on your back. You've kissed me so much that now I want to kiss you.'

He reached out for her. Firmly she put his hands behind his head. 'Lie there, I said. I know what I want from us, see if you do, too. Now…' Her head bent over him and again there was that gasp of pleasure.

Once, twice he tried to move his hands and she put them back behind his head. Then, moments, minutes later she heard him pant, 'I think…now…before it is too late…'

'Yes, now,' she said, and pulled him over onto her. 'Yes, now, Adam…now…' She could hear her own voice rising, hear the half scream of passion, hear his growl of delight. 'Now, Adam…now. Oh, please… Now!'

Then all was done. They lay there panting side by side, feeling their bodies covered with the warmth of ecstasy, feeling their heartbeats slowly returning to normal.

'That was—' he started, but she leaned over to kiss him silent.

'That was so much that talking about it will do no good,' she said. 'So now we can sleep.' And they slept.

CHAPTER EIGHT

AMY woke first. It was dark and still early. For a moment she lay there, remembering last night and the comfort of lying next to Adam's body since then. He was breathing heavily, still asleep. Lightly she kissed him on the shoulder, then wriggled out of bed.

She made them both mugs of tea then gently shook him awake. There was light in the sky, they had things to do. 'Soon you must go,' she said.

He sat up, took the tea then kissed her on the cheek. 'Last night was—' he started, but she interrupted.

'Adam, last night was last night. Now it is over. Now I have a daughter, you have a daughter and they're probably both coming over here soon. We both have responsibilities, work to do.'

'But things are different now,' he said. 'We have things to decide.'

She didn't expect it, it came out of the blue.

But calmly he said, 'Amy, I love you.'

There was silence in the room. She felt lost, dismayed, not sure what to think. How could she cope with this? It had been the last thing she had anticipated. She said, 'Suddenly things in my life are changing. That was a declaration. It needs, deserves an answer. And I'm not sure what to say.'

He smiled, kissed her gently. 'It's quite easy, quite simple,' he said. 'Three little words, or perhaps four. I love you, too. There's no need to plan the future, to work out what might happen. Just say them then take as long as you like to decide on the future. Only three words. I love you. And, Amy, when I said them, I never meant anything more in my life.'

She looked around in bewilderment. This was her bedroom, always a haven, a place of safety and comfort. And now she was lost in it. She knew this was not a good time to make decisions, when she was naked, his warm body next to hers, her body aching for him again. What did she want? At the moment she wanted him. She desperately wanted to spend the rest of her life with him. But caution told her—

The telephone by the side of her bed rang.

'Leave it,' he said.

She shook her head. 'Only important people know this number,' she said, and lifted the receiver. 'Hi, Johanne.' She saw Adam's eyes roll. 'Yes, wonderful time, thank you... Yes I think your dad enjoyed it, too...' She pushed away the hand that was stroking her breast. 'That's really nice for them, and he'll drop you off here... Yes, still in bed but I'll be up by the time you get here. Bye, love.'

She turned to Adam and said, 'Noel phoned early, he wants to take Ma out. He's volunteering to drive Johanne and Elizabeth back here first. They'll be arriving in about half an hour.'

He smiled painfully. 'And you want me to go? I suppose I ought to, but do I get an answer first?'

'No way can I give you any kind of an answer, think of anything to say when we're both liable to be caught by your daughter in our underwear.' Quickly, she kissed him. 'Adam, having them come here isn't what I want. But get dressed and go.'

He sat there a moment, then nodded judiciously. 'Perhaps you're right. But I want an answer some time.'

He dressed quickly. She, still in her robe, cleared up from the night before. Then he was at the front door, his shirt creased, his tie not on. And he still looked gorgeous. 'Amy, I'll say it again. I love you.' A quick last kiss and he was gone.

She peered at him through the closed curtains, saw his car draw away. Then she sighed. She had thinking to do. But before she could start, Johanne and Elizabeth arrived.

There were always things to do on a Sunday, it was a busy day. But in the afternoon Johanne took Elizabeth for a walk in the park and she phoned Adam. 'I just want to thank you for a lovely evening...'

'And a wonderful night,' he added. 'How are you feeling?'

She was honest. 'Very mixed up,' she said. 'I'm feeling all sorts of emotions, and I'm trying to unravel them. Last night made me feel happier than I can remember...but there's more to life than that. And this morning, what you said, it shocked me. But I don't know why it did.'

'I know. Think about me, sweetheart, I think about you.'

'Give me time. I need a bit more time. But not a lot.' Then she rang off.

She had thought about him non-stop for the rest of the weekend. On Monday morning she had slipped into his office before the patients had been due, had

walked to where he had been sitting behind his desk
and kissed him. 'I just can't say it yet,' she told him.
'I know that it's true that I…that I…but, Adam, I just
can't say it yet. And I want to, I need to. Can you
give me a couple more days? Do you think I'm being
silly?'

'Never silly,' he said. 'And I know you're worth
waiting for.'

She thought of something they could do together,
she wanted just to spend time with him. Peter Brooks
was back at home now. And after an awkward start
he and Nancy seemed to be growing closer together.
Peter was still ill, but he was a much more likable
man than he had been.

She told Adam this and went on, 'I'd like you to
come and talk to them both. You need to examine
Peter and it's good to see him so different.'

'Fair enough. I fancy a trip out into the country
with you.'

'This is business, not pleasure!'

'Who could think it could be anything else?' She
could almost believe he was as hurt as his voice suggested—until she saw him smile.

It was a late autumn day, clear but cold. They set
off in her car, both enjoying the ride. Soon they were
in the countryside, the familiar landscape of green
hills and white limestone walls.

Amy heard a buzzing somewhere near and slowed
down, knowing what it would be. A moment later
both of them jerked. A quad bike suddenly leapt over
the ditch by the side of the road. It bounced clear of
the ground in front of them and set off like an enraged

bee up the fellside. The driver turned and waved at them. It seemed an incredibly steep hill to climb.

'Are those things safe?' asked Adam. 'I've seen them a lot. And that driver is acting like a lunatic.'

'They're very handy on farms,' Amy said. 'They can get where a tractor can't, are supposed to be safer than a motorbike. A lot of people have them, they're handy for rounding up sheep and so on. The trouble is, they're fun to drive. And to take chances with.'

He nodded. 'I'm still a boy at heart, I'd like to try one myself. But I'd wear a helmet. Not like that young man.'

She grinned. 'A shepherd with a helmet instead of a crook?' It was good to be out with him, talking easily, joking with each other. They did get on so well together, in all sorts of ways.

But she frowned. There was something wrong. Something digging at the edge of her consciousness, something she had forgotten or something wrong. What?

He noticed her frown. 'Problems?' he asked.

'I don't know, I'm not sure.' She pulled into the side of the road, turned off the engine. Then she had it. 'Listen! That quad bike that we saw. We can still hear the engine.'

'True. Noisy things, aren't they?'

'No, listen. When you hear those things the engine note goes up and down all the time, because they're always changing speed. But that engine note has been the same for the past five minutes.'

They both listened, it was true. 'Suggesting?' he asked, though she knew he knew what she meant.

'The quad is stuck somewhere, somehow. And the driver can't turn off the engine.'

'Probably nothing. But it's a fine day, and we have some time. Let's go for a little walk.'

She drove back to where the quad bike had raced up the fellside and parked her car. Then they both set off to climb upwards. She noticed Adam carried his doctor's bag with him. He was worried, too. Or just being careful.

It was a hard slog upwards. The hill was steep, little edges of limestone protruding, sheep running away, baaing. Soon she was out of breath, her uniform sticking to her. Adam was obviously fit. Other than loosening his tie, he showed no sign of fatigue. He took her hand to help her upwards, and she liked it.

But they were now both apprehensive. The screaming of the engine got louder, the note remained the same. And they got to the top of the fell.

There was a path running along the ridge. The side they had climbed had the gentler slope. The other side of the fell dropped precipitously downwards, then there was a sheer cliff dropping to the river. A dangerous place.

They saw the quad bike first. It was upturned, four wheels uselessly in the air, on the edge of a little shelf about four feet below the path. Its engine was still howling and they could see it vibrating, stones rattling downwards from under it. Just below the quad bike was the outstretched figure of the rider. He didn't move, apparently unconscious. Amy shivered. It wasn't a good place to be. If he moved, he could roll right down the slope.

Adam shouted, 'He must have tried to ride along

the path and tipped over. I'll see what we can do for him, you phone for an ambulance. This is beyond us, we need paramedics.'

Clutching his bag, he scrambled down as Amy stayed on the ridge to phone. She gave precise instructions, explaining that her car would mark the best place for the ambulance to stop. Then she moved down to join Adam.

He had turned off the engine of the bike, it was easier to think and talk when the constant screaming had stopped. Then he had started to carefully examine the driver. Stones slipped from under Amy's feet as she came alongside Adam.

'ABC is fine,' he muttered. 'No immediate problem with his breathing or circulation.' He pointed to a bloody wound on the man's head. 'I think he's concussed. Get a pad out and put it over that, will you, Amy? Then we'll slip a hard collar on him, just in case. He should have worn a helmet!'

'Tell him that when he comes to,' said Amy as she deftly applied one of the dressings from the bag. 'What about the spine? Was he thrown onto the rock or did he roll onto it?'

Adam shrugged. 'No way of telling yet. He needs…'

There was a rattling noise. A few stones rolled down towards them, one or two landing on the rider's body. They looked up. The quad bike was right above them, balanced very precariously on the edge of the little platform.

Adam said, 'I think we'll risk injuring the spine and ease him a couple of feet to the—'

Then it all seemed to happen in slow motion—

though it must have been very fast indeed. More stones rattled down towards them, some of them quite big. They looked up at the quad bike and saw that it had slipped another few inches, was, in fact, coming over the edge of the platform. It was going to roll towards them and land on them.

Amy saw the indecision on Adam's face, and then that determined look that she had seen so often before. First he pushed her, violently, so she fell on her back, winded but out of harm's way. Then, just as the bike was about to land on him and the rider, he lunged at it and tried to push it to one side so it would miss them. And, somehow, he succeeded.

Amy was desperately trying to drag air into her lungs. But she heard him gasp, then saw the quad bike roll and bounce down the hillside, to disappear out of sight. She could breathe a little easier now. She looked at Adam.

Now there were two unconscious figures.

She was probably bruised a bit and shaken quite a lot, but there appeared to be nothing seriously wrong with her. Still, rather than stand upright, she crawled over to Adam's unconscious body, afraid of what she might find. She had to stay calm!

He was breathing. ABC checked. Blood streaked across his face, another nasty head wound. Then her eyes widened in horror. There was a dark stain on the torn shoulder of his jacket that grew as she looked at it. She grabbed a pair of scissors from the bag and cut away all the fabric, exposing a great gash high on his arm. Blood pulsed out from the wound, the brachial artery had been severed. Adam was bleeding to death.

Quickly, Amy took a couple of pads and pushed them hard down on the wound. She then dragged his body round so his arm was as high as it would go, harder for the heart to pump blood out.

Keeping up the direct pressure, she took out her phone and dialled the emergency services again to tell them there were now two casualties, one with a torn artery, with resultant rapid blood loss. Calmly, the woman on the phone tried to tell her what to do. 'I'm a nurse,' Amy cut in, 'I know what to do. Just get the ambulance here. Please hurry.'

Monitoring Adam's vital signs, Amy felt lonely, lost. She knew that in an injury there always seemed to be more blood than there really was—but, even so, there seemed to be a vast amount. She changed the pads as blood began to seep through the first set, and looked at Adam's face. It was white—of course. Too white?

Again with one hand she managed to dial a number, got through to the surgery. Rita recognised the urgency in her voice at once, fetched Dr Wright out of a consultation. Amy told him where she was, what had happened to Adam and the quad rider. Talking to him calmed her a little. He told her what she already knew—that she was doing the only things possible. Then he said he'd see what he could do to speed up the ambulance—but they both knew that all that could be done had been done.

She rang off, looked down at Adam. There was a limit to the amount of blood a body could lose. She remembered that the average person had approximately five litres of blood. Lose two litres and you would die.

Concentrate! Had she heard the distant sound of an ambulance siren? That had been some time ago. She didn't dare hope or think, she just concentrated on her fingers, tried to keep the blood from escaping. She now needed to grab for another set of pads. Blood was starting to ooze through the ones she had.

It came as a surprise. There were voices, shockingly near. One said, 'All right, love, there's help here, we'll be right with you.' She looked up, saw two men carefully climbing down towards her, dressed in fluorescent green coats. One held a large bag, the other carried a stretcher.

As she looked another two men arrived, similarly dressed. Someone put an arm around her, helped her to stand as another man thrust a fresh pad onto Adam's bleeding arm. She was helped to the path and someone wrapped a blanket round her then asked if she was OK.

'I'm fine, fine, I'm a nurse.' She dragged her thoughts together, then gave a concise account of what had happened, what she and Adam had done. Case histories in accidents were important. 'You will let me know how he is,' she pleaded.

'We'll do what we can.'

It was even harder sitting there on the path, doing nothing, than it had been trying to keep Adam alive. But she knew the best thing to do was to keep away, to leave everything to the experts. As she thought this, two of the paramedics climbed up to her, carrying the quad driver, now strapped into a stretcher. How was Adam?

Shockingly, she found herself thinking of her dead husband. She remembered sitting by his bed, knowing that he would never recover, would probably soon die. She hadn't loved him, all feeling for him had gone. But she remembered wondering what it would be like if she did still love him. How would she feel? Well, now she thought she knew. She couldn't take any more hurt. She loved Adam! Why hadn't she told him so? And another thought struck her, so horrible as to be almost unthinkable. What if it was now too late?

She wanted to scream with horror. But years of training, years of observing accidents had taught her one thing above all others. Panic was always wrong, often dangerous.

She looked down the side of the fell, there was an ambulance there, her own car and, to her surprise, another one. And climbing up towards her was Dr Wright.

He reached her, panting. She said, knowing that her voice was faltering, 'Adam's lost a lot of blood. Will you see how he is?'

He glanced down and said, 'The paramedics are doing a great job. Now, let's look at you.'

It was the swiftest of examinations, but at the end of it he said, 'I think you'll be fine. Now, wait here and then I'll get you down.'

'But Adam! I want to go to hospital with him and I—'

'Just sit here a minute,' he soothed. 'Adam's being looked after by the experts.'

He went and had a quick word with the paramedics and then came back to say, 'They've got a drip into him, his condition's stabilised but it's important that they get him to hospital as quickly as possible. Now,

I'm your doctor and I'm telling you that you are going home. You can do nothing for Adam at the hospital. Nothing yet.'

'Is he going to die?' Was that nearly hysterical voice hers? She didn't want an answer but she had to ask.

Ever the professional, Dr Wright answered carefully. 'He's lost a lot of blood, but he's a strong, fit man. I think we can be hopeful.'

As he spoke she saw the paramedics climb up onto the path, Adam between them strapped to the stretcher. She caught one glimpse of his face. Then the paramedics set off down. 'Let's go home, then,' she said.

There were things to do. She was taken home, told to have a bath and then go to bed. Dr Wright examined her again, winced at the bruises that he found and made her take a sedative. After her repeated requests he phoned the hospital and was told that Adam's condition was dangerous but not critical. When it was possible he would go into surgery to have the torn artery repaired. The scalp wound wasn't serious. And the driver of the quad bike was doing fine. Dr Wright phoned Sylvia and arranged for Elizabeth to be looked after overnight. He phoned the school, arranged for Johanne to be brought home.

There was just too much emotion, too much to think about and too little Amy could do. She loved Adam and she'd never told him so. And now perhaps it could be too…no, she wouldn't, couldn't think that. But after a while, perhaps because of the sedative, Amy slept.

*   *   *

Amy had worked in a hospital, had done her share of comforting. She had reassured anxious relatives about the state of their loved ones. But she had never actually experienced the combination of terror and boredom there was in waiting. There was nothing she could do. That evening she, Johanne and Dr Wright sat there and drank plastic cups of coffee and waited and hoped.

The surgeon came to talk to them. He said the operation would be difficult—the gash was deep, there were tears in the artery wall. They were still pumping blood into him, but the surgeon felt reasonably confident. Adam would have to convalese, of course, but in time all should be well.

He looked at Amy approvingly. 'Good thing you were with him and you were a nurse. You saved his life, you know.'

Johanne burst into tears and threw her arms around Amy. The surgeon blinked.

More waiting, perhaps two hours. And then the surgeon returned, a beaming smile on his face. 'Done,' he said. 'And though I say so myself, a pretty good job, too. Of course, there's always the chance of complications but there should be no trouble now.'

'Can we see him?' Johanne quavered.

'You certainly can. But you'll not get much sense out of him.'

Amy knew this was possibly not a good idea for Johanne. People fresh out of surgery seldom looked their best. But they went anyway.

Adam managed to smile at them, touched Johanne's hand. Amy leaned over him, kissed him on the forehead. Then his eyes shut and he drifted into unconsciousness. The nurse suggested that they might like to wait till the morning, he'd be in a better state then. So they left.

Dr Wright insisted that Amy take a couple of days off, so the next day she took Johanne to the hospital. Adam was pale but otherwise apparently fine. There was a heavy dressing on his arm, a smaller one on his head. And he was pleased to see them both.

Johanne kissed him first, but very cautiously tried not to touch him. 'I'm all right,' he told her. 'You can hug me if you want.' So she did, and then burst into tears again.

Then Amy leaned over to kiss him. Just a friendly kiss, because Johanne was there and they didn't want to start her thinking. Not quite yet. But she felt for his hand and squeezed it, and she knew he knew what she meant.

There were cards and flowers from the surgery, all wishing him well. He had already seen the surgeon, who was very pleased with his progress. They were planning his discharge already. 'He asked if there was a good district nurse to look after me,' Adam said with a grin.

'Not me,' Amy said. 'No way will I be your nurse. But I'll come round and cook your meals.'

'No, I will,' Johanne said. 'I want to come home now, Dad, and look after you. Though I'll be sorry to leave Amy and Elizabeth.'

'We'll work something out,' Adam said. 'But I'd rather have you at school than acting as a nurse. In fact, I suspect I'll be quite capable of looking after myself. Or I might find some other solution.'

He was looking at Amy as he said this, and she knew the secret message he was trying to get across.

'You'll have a lot of help, I'm sure,' she said. 'And I'll do everything you want—everything.'

When he smiled back at her she knew he had got her message.

Johanne was with Adam every time Amy visited Adam. But the next day she managed to sneak a couple of minutes alone with him. She started by kissing him properly.

'I thought I might lose you and my life seemed worthless,' she whispered. 'So I'm asking for a second chance. Now isn't a good time. But when you're better, I want you to tell me that you love me again. Then we'll start from the beginning again. Well, from after when you spent the night at my house. Is that a good idea?'

'I'm feeling better already,' he said. 'Will you kiss me again before Johanne comes back?'

She and Johanne visited every night until he was sent home to his flat. Then Johanne went to join him, and Amy visited most nights anyway. Johanne was a real helper—which meant that Adam and Amy didn't have too much time alone together. Amy thought this was probably a good thing as it was not a good time to make decisions. But he knew what she felt. And from time to time he looked at her, and she gave him a secret smile because she knew what he was feeling, too.

She knew some men just couldn't take illness or

injury—they showed a side of themselves that no one had suspected. Adam wasn't like this, he was a perfect patient. Occasionally Amy suspected he was in pain, but he never said anything, was never short-tempered. And she loved him more and more. Nothing had been said so far, but that didn't matter. Now she knew they had time.

There was one last problem, one last obstacle she had to surmount, and it came as a shock. As she picked up Elizabeth one evening, her mother casually handed her a carrier bag. 'I found this upstairs. It's yours, I think. I must have picked it up when you were moving into your new house.'

Amy peered inside the carrier—and thought her heart would stop. There was an old cigar box. She recognised it at once, it was hers. Fortunately her mother was putting on Elizabeth's coat and she didn't notice just how upset Amy was—and Amy managed to conceal it.

It was to be an ordinary evening. For once she wasn't calling round to see Adam, he was having other visitors. So she gave Elizabeth her tea, bathed her and read the necessary story, waited till she was asleep. And all the time she was aware of the cigar box waiting for her. Finally, when she couldn't think of any more tasks to occupy her, she sat and stretched out a trembling hand to open the box.

After her husband had died she had thrown away everything of his that she could. She had even thrown away all the photographs they had had taken together. Then she had taken all his clothes, his books and his CDs and put them in four large boxes. Dr Wright had come and taken them away, given them to a charity. Amy had just wanted to get rid of them. But somehow this cigar box had survived. She knew she should burn it, unopened. But she couldn't.

She had hated the smell of cigars in the house, Paul had smoked them just to show her who was boss. But she had liked the box, it was handsome, made of cedar. So she had kept it, stored things in it. She opened the box.

There were two sets of letters, one set tied in pink ribbon, one set tied in blue. Amy sat there and stared at them.

When they had been engaged they had been apart, she working in a hospital in Sheffield, he working as a salesman, wandering round the country. She had written to him—sometimes every day. He hadn't written back as often and his letters had been much shorter.

For a while they had been so much in love.

When they had married he had shown her how he had kept all her letters as she had kept his, and had suggested that she should keep the two sets together. And she had done so.

Now, with a sick feeling, she untied the bundles and started to read. They were in order, she could follow lines of thought.

Paul had written a good letter. But, then, he always had been silver-tongued, persuasive, a brilliant salesman. Which was why he had managed to con her for so long. After they had married she had felt guilty of suspecting him when she had found obvious signs of other women on his clothes. He had sounded so hurt! But these letters dated from before then.

How they had planned! Where to buy their house, what furniture to get first. Where they would go for their holidays. And the long, long letters planning her wedding.

She shook herself. She had just read a letter from him professing his love for her. It sounded so marvellous, she remembered it making her so happy. And it had all been false. She dropped the letters back in the box.

It was surprisingly easy to do. She found she just didn't care. She took the box downstairs, emptied the letters onto the fire. Then she stirred the ashes until all the paper was consumed. The ashes of love? Nothing like it.

She sat there for perhaps fifteen minutes and then smiled. She went upstairs, reached into her bedside cabinet for the photograph of her with Adam. When it was time she intended to have it enlarged, keep it proudly on her dressing-table.

Burning the letters had been the last step she needed to take. The last ghost was laid, now she was free. She could tell Adam that she loved him, that her past was over. Now all there was in her life was a future.

CHAPTER NINE

'NOEL asked me, I accepted, we're going to get married,' Sylvia said. 'Look, he's given me a ring. It's an emerald.'

It was early one evening and Amy had called to pick up Elizabeth. Now she looked at her mother, not making sense of what she had just heard. Then she threw her arms around her mother. 'Ma, I'm so happy for you. I think he's a lovely man and I think he'll make you very happy.'

Then she stepped back, looked critically at her mother. 'How long has this been going on?'

'Quite a while. He's been hinting for long enough, but never quite spoken out. Said he didn't want to spoil what we had. And I was happy with things, too. I did intend to ask your advice, but after your ex-husband I thought you were against all marriages.'

'You didn't have to worry. I'd have said yes, encouraged you,' Amy protested. 'I've seen that smile on your face, that gleam in your eye—but I never thought you'd go this far.' She thought. 'But you've been not married for a long time now. Aren't you bothered that your life is going to change?'

Her mother shrugged. 'I am a bit. But if you see something good—you go for it. I was very happy with your dad. Noel knows that, he was happy, too. So why can't we be happy with each other?'

'No reason at all. I think it's great. Can Elizabeth be a bridesmaid?'

'Who else? And you can be a matron of honour.'

Her mother paused, and then said diffidently, 'I'd like it if you got married, too, Amy. To the right man, of course.'

'I might like it myself,' Amy said with a grin. 'Let's just see what happens, shall we?' And beyond that she would not be drawn.

Perhaps it was chance, perhaps in some way it was ordained. But Adam phoned her next morning.

'I've decided I'm officially better,' he said on the phone. 'I've also decided that if I stay in any longer I'll go mad. I'm going out for a walk. Would you like to meet me?'

'You sound better,' Amy said, 'but it's a wet miserable morning. Are you sure you ought to be out? I could come and pick you up.'

'If I see you, the sun will be shining. How about by the river in half an hour?'

'I'll be there,' she said. 'Hey, Adam?'

'Yes?' Still a little doubt in his voice.

'It's good to hear you sounding so well.' Then she rang off.

It was a Saturday morning. Elizabeth was with Sylvia—they were off on a shopping expedition to Sheffield to buy a bridesmaid's outfit. Amy had intended to call on Adam but this made it much easier.

She saw him sitting on a bench in a shelter, the rain dripping from the roof. She sat by him and kissed him, the long kiss of a lover. His face was thinner, but he was still gorgeous.

He spoke first. 'I've been thinking,' he said. 'I'm getting better every day. Soon I'll be able to start light work. But I've been thinking about my life in general, nearly dying and then having to spend a long time in bed makes you think.'

'I thought about Johanne and now I know where I was going wrong. I was being selfish.' He grinned. 'You know, last night I practically had to force her out of the house to see her boyfriend. She said she wanted to stay in and look after me. And she's out with him right now.'

'You're lucky in her,' said Amy. 'I hope my daughter grows up like her.'

He reached over to squeeze her hand, then let it go.

'You saved my life,' he said. 'Don't argue, we both know it's true.' He smiled. 'I heard a Chinese saying that if you save someone's life, you are responsible for them for the rest of that life. What a responsibility for you!'

'I can take it,' Amy said cheerfully. 'I want to take it.'

'We had a holiday romance. But I thought it might become something much more than that. I wondered if I should do as you suggested—just keep it as a memory. My experience of long-term relationships—with my wife—didn't do much to encourage me. But I came here to see you. I told you when I came that I wanted to see what would happen. A lot has happened. Like I said, you helped me with Johanne, I learned more about work, there was the night of the dance which I will never forget. Then I told you I loved you. I thought that all would be well then—but then came the accident. And I'm glad you were there for me and I'm glad that we agreed to leave things till I was better.'

He took both her hands, pulled her to him and kissed her. 'I love you, Amy,' he said. 'I want us to have a future together. I've thought about this non-stop over the past few days, you are what I want so desperately. So I'm making my declaration again. Can you do the same?'

'Adam, of course I can! I love— Adam, what's the matter?' He was gazing over her shoulder, his expression horrified.

'I don't believe it,' he muttered. 'This just can't happen to us. Not now.'

Amy turned to look. There, coming towards them, was Johanne. She was holding the hand of her boy-friend. 'Hi, Dad,' she shouted. 'Glad we've found you. Jack's parents have asked if I want to go round there for a meal tonight so if you're up to being on your own, I thought—'

'Great idea,' said Amy. 'Your dad's coming round to have dinner with me. Aren't you, Adam?'

'Oh. Yes,' said Adam.

Amy took pains with the supper. For too long she had been living off sandwiches and hasty meals grabbed when it had been convenient. This time she wanted to be at ease, to be gracious.

She bought salads, cold meats, a wonderful bread from the small local baker. And a fresh fruit salad. The Burgundy was a bottle specially recommended by her friend in the wine shop. The table was set almost formally, for two—Elizabeth was staying at her mother's house tonight. No strong light, the room would be illuminated by candles. Then it was time to change.

She bathed then consciously and deliberately put on the frilly underwear. A pink dress, formal but pretty. And then she lit the candles and sat down to wait.

Adam looked well when he came in. Black trousers and leather jacket, a white shirt. No tie, of course. And he brought flowers and more wine.

'The last time I was in this room I had been so happy,' he said, 'and as I left I told you that I loved you.'

'So you did. And I think you might get an answer tonight.' Then she frowned. 'Adam, I'm sorry but this morning, when Johanne turned up out of the blue, I was going to—'

'Hey! No one wants to hear a romantic declaration in front of his daughter. Or a hurried one.'

He looked at the candles, the sparking glasses and cutlery. Then he looked at her in her pink dress. 'This is much more inviting,' he said. 'Now I'm happy to be here.'

'I'm happy, too,' she said. 'More happy than you can think. And we've got time.'

He looked at her thoughtfully, but she was mischievous and avoided his eye. 'Give me your coat and then we'll eat,' she said. 'I'm starving.'

They had a pleasant, relaxed meal. They talked about Sylvia and Noel getting married, about what subjects Johanne should take at school, about whether the town should have a bypass. It was easy, casual conversation. They had all evening. They had each other.

Eventually the meal ended and they found themselves sitting side by side on her couch. She kicked off her shoes, put her feet across his lap. And when she reached for her glass she found that the wine had run out. She blinked. Had they drunk an entire bottle? 'I've got another bottle here,' she said. 'I bought it for tonight.'

He reached for the corkscrew, opened the bottle, tasted the wine. 'This is fantastic,' he said. 'This wine is worth a toast.'

'The wine was specially recommended,' she told him. 'I wanted something to…to mark the occasion.'

'The occasion?'

She leaned over, clinked her glass against his. 'This is an occasion. Now I know, now I'm certain, my old life is behind me. And I've something to say that I've been waiting to say for days. I love you, Adam Ross. You can make me happier than I've ever been before. And I'll make you happy, too.'

He put down his glass, gathered her into his arms. 'And how I love you, Amy Harrison. We'll make each other happy.' He kissed her. Then he smiled. 'Maybe we can start now…'

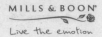

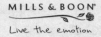
_Medical
romance™

THE DOCTOR'S TENDER SECRET *by Kate Hardy*

(London City General)

On the hectic paediatrics ward of London City General, love just isn't running smoothly for Dr Brad Hutton and Dr Zoe Kennedy. They may be instantly smitten with each other once again, but the secrets they have kept locked away make their future together uncertain. For Brad, the solution lies in putting his past behind him. But Zoe's secret goes a lot deeper…

AIRBORNE EMERGENCY *by Olivia Gates*

(Air Rescue)

Surgeon Cassandra St James couldn't wait to join the Global Aid Organisation's flying Jet Hospital – until she encountered mission leader Vidal Santiago. What was this millionaire plastic surgeon – the man she loved and loathed – doing on a humanitarian mission? Had she misjudged him? And could she control the unwanted passion that flared between them?

OUTBACK DOCTOR IN DANGER *by Emily Forbes*

When an explosion rocks a peaceful Outback town, flying doctor Matt Zeller is on hand to help. He hasn't been emotionally close to anyone for years, and has dedicated himself to his work – then he meets Nurse Steffi Harrison at the scene. She's due to stay in town for just a few weeks – but after knowing her for mere moments Matt knows he wants her to stay!

On sale 7th January 2005

Available at most branches of WHSmith, Tesco, ASDA, Martins, Borders, Eason, Sainsbury's and all good paperback bookshops.

No. 1 *New York Times* bestselling author

NORA ROBERTS

presents two classic novels about the walls people build around their hearts and how to break them down...

Love by Design

Available from 21st January 2005

FREE!

4 Books
and a surprise gift!

We would like to take this opportunity to thank you for reading this Mills & Boon® book by offering you the chance to take FOUR more specially selected titles from the Medical Romance™ series absolutely FREE! We're also making this offer to introduce you to the benefits of the Reader Service™—

- ★ **FREE home delivery**
- ★ **FREE gifts and competitions**
- ★ **FREE monthly Newsletter**
- ★ **Exclusive Reader Service offers**
- ★ **Books available before they're in the shops**

Accepting these FREE books and gift places you under no obligation to buy, you may cancel at any time, even after receiving your free shipment. Simply complete your details below and return the entire page to the address below. You don't even need a stamp!

YES! Please send me 4 free Medical Romance books and a surprise gift. I understand that unless you hear from me, I will receive 6 superb new titles every month for just £2.69 each, postage and packing free. I am under no obligation to purchase any books and may cancel my subscription at any time. The free books and gift will be mine to keep in any case.

M4ZEF

Ms/Mrs/Miss/Mr ....Initials...
                                                                                                    BLOCK CAPITALS PLEASE

Surname...

Address...

....

....Postcode ....

Send this whole page to:
UK: FREEPOST CN81, Croydon, CR9 3WZ